The Eternal Echo

The Eternal Echo

Jeff Musillo

A Strawberry Book
www.strawberrybooks.com

SB

Strawberry Books is a publishing house that thrills, delights and informs our
readers with high-quality e-books, physical books and online content.

Please check out our website and follow us on Twitter:

@thrillsdelights

Dedicated to Karen,
for introducing me to Dr. Ravensdale

Table of Contents

Prologue

I felt a wave of emotions when it all took place. A friend of mine had died. Her name was Karen.

She was a family friend first. My mother's friend. But over time I had the opportunity to know and appreciate her, so I was heartbroken over her passing.

But I also experienced a feeling of extreme curiosity and excitement. This was due to what she left me in her will.

I've published the books The Ease of Access, Can You See That Sound, Snapshot Americana, and The States. But I hit a wall following those releases. I wanted to write a horror novel but was unable to develop new material. This was upsetting.

Prior to her death, I expressed to Karen my concerns about the writer's block. She tried helping me whenever possible. She was a psychiatrist and would occasionally offer little yet nonspecific stories regarding her patients. Never too many details, given the whole Physician-patient privilege, but some pieces here and there. She hoped to inspire some creativity.

Her stories did indeed spark something in me to write a short story or two, although I was still having problems with the novel.

Throughout her stories Karen also generated my incredible interest in one of her patients: Dr. David Ravensdale.

Dr. Ravensdale was (and still is) incarcerated, so heavily imprisoned in fact that he was only allowed out of his cell for psychotherapy sessions with Karen.

The more Karen told me about this man the more difficult it was for me to stop thinking about him. I wanted to know anything and everything about the person newspapers had branded: "The most dangerous serial killer of the 21st Century."

But Karen could only provide so much information.

That is until she passed.

I eventually discovered that Dr. Ravensdale started writing his own story as soon as he was incarcerated.

Mere weeks before her death, the Doctor gave Karen the manuscript and told her, "Whatever true story you need to know is in these pages."

For the rest of her life, Karen studied and utilized the manuscript and even included her own records and questions from her sessions with Dr. Ravensdale.

This manuscript is what she left me in her will. Along with a note that said: "This might help."

I was ecstatic. I felt I could finally become inspired enough by Dr. Ravensdale's story to start creating my new novel.

This didn't happen.

When I finished reading Dr. Ravensdale's story, which is his analysis of the horrible events he personally created, I realized there was very little I could do. What I read had disturbed me and stuck with me so much that I knew my own writing on the subject would feel like replication.

But still, I had to do something.

The story had to be seen.

So I arranged everything with my publisher and took it upon myself to type out the entire manuscript and even edit some sections in order to make the Doctor's story more comprehensible, especially since there were a few unreasonable, sometimes nonsensical, rants that went on for at least twenty pages at a clip.

I also made sure to keep Karen's notes in the story. There are fifteen of these notes throughout the book and they are labeled and italicized.

Although I did not write this story, the one Dr. Ravensdale himself titled, *The Eternal Echo*, I'm still thrilled to play a part in getting it seen.

By no means should this man be celebrated. He is an awful individual and deserves every available punishment.

Yet I still believe his story should be read.

Plenty have heard about him and his atrocities in the news, but this story is from his own point of view, and I believe it is this perspective that makes the story whole.

So please allow me to stop my own writing and present the man himself.

Dr. David Ravensdale.

The Eternal Echo

I – My Location

Please pardon my writing. I realize it's sloppy. Just know that it has taken me some time to make my script legible. It was no easy task. It still isn't. I am aware of no one else with this ability to write with their mouth.

I'm left with no other choice, you see. This godawful straightjacket eliminates the chance for me to write like a human being. This godawful straightjacket!

Why is this happening?

I feel there is no reason for me to be here. There is definitely no reason for my arms to be bound. No reason for this restriction.

Unfortunately, the powers to be at this "correctional facility," my current home, do not feel the same.

This is because they do not understand. None of them understand. Not the management or the guards of this institution. Not the news journalists. Not the judge or the jury members or anyone else present in that court room. Especially not the family members of the "victims."

No one understands what I've actually done. They just *think* I'm a monster. But believing something doesn't always bring about the truth.

And what is the truth?

The truth is that they can't comprehend the significance of my life's work.

But I can't be too upset.

When it comes to immediacy, I understand that genius is seldom recognized. It can take decades, sometimes centuries, for true genius to be appreciated.

Hence all of these…misunderstandings. Hence my incarceration. Hence me being in a straightjacket. Hence my having to write by clamping down my teeth and lips on this gnarled pencil and working my neck until it is sore and nearly too tight to move.

How did I get to this point?

I believe this writing process all began as a joke. A cruel joke by my guards. Or at least an attempt at one.

Some time ago, I asked one of the guards for writing materials. I had a momentary lapse of awareness and forgot I was incapacitated, to say the least. I forgot I was not exactly free to write like normal. The guard laughed at me and left me in my padded cell. He returned the following day with a notebook and this mangled pencil.

I sometimes wish the guard had given me a pen. The pencil sometimes breaks and I have to use my teeth and the sturdiness of the cement floor to sharpen the tip. I've had many splinters in my mouth. They have been quite painful. But I know better than to ask for a pen. I know that a question of that nature would lead to the guard seizing my possessions. I certainly know that. You see, I am still of sound mind.

***

The name of this institution is The Hera Correctional Facility. For the foreseeable future, I am located in an area dedicated to the imprisonment and mental evaluation of "violent criminals".

I do not believe I am a violent criminal.

Yes, I took what some might call questionable measures for my experiment to progress. This is true. But I do not believe this makes me a bad person.

How could I be a violent criminal? I'm a man who has saved lives. I'm also a man who has given life! I have donated blood and I have donated sperm. I have donated a great deal of sperm. For all I know I could be a creator!

So no. I do not believe I am a violent criminal.

But when it comes to the viewpoints of others, my beliefs don't matter. This is why I am here. This is why I've been incarcerated for the past one hundred eighty-two hours, forty-seven minutes, and eleven seconds.

You see that? Do you see the sharpness of my mind? Of my memory? No one at this institution tells me the date. None of the guards. Not the warden. Not even these so-called Doctors.

I don't need them to tell me anything! My mind is beyond quick. I forget nothing. Even if I have essentially been in the same room for one hundred ninety-four hours, twenty-seven minutes, and eleven seconds.

How could I not have a good memory? I am who I am! The falsely imprisoned, highly misunderstood Dr. David Ravensdale.

II – Me

I was born in 1957. Grew up in South London. I didn't initially exist in what could be referred to as a blissful environment. I was born into financial security, which was helpful, but that's hardly ever the end all be all.

My father, Everett Ravensdale, was an esteemed Doctor who made a great income. Like father, like son.

I didn't have a mother in my life. If I were forced to locate faults in my character, I'd say that perhaps the absence of a mother hurt my development of a tender attitude.

NOTE #1
KAREN: *Are there moments in your life where you wish you were more kindhearted?*
DR. RAVENSDALE: *Absolutely not. I've grown to learn that there is no room in this world for sympathy. I've met many kindhearted individuals in my time, and guess what, most of them are no longer breathing.*
KAREN: *Who are you referring to?*
DR. RAVENSDALE: *You know exactly who I'm referring to. And you know that none of them were as strong as me.*

I was told while growing up that my mother had died giving birth to me. I believed this to be true since my father was the one who told me. I figured he wouldn't lie to me, at least not about something like that. I also believed the story since death during childbirth happened frequently enough back then. It was like nature's way of getting rid of the weak.

But as I was approaching my adult years, while attending medical school at Cambridge, my father let me in on a little family secret.

He was on his deathbed when he revealed the truth. On his final breaths as a matter of fact. I took leave from the university to be by his side. I remember thinking that I was by his side more out of duty than out of desire. We were family, yet we never cared for one another. Not emotionally.

At my father's very end, it was just him and I in a bright and cold room. The type of room I would see many years later. I've grown to hate rooms like that.

With great struggle he beckoned me to move closer. Closer. Closer. I did as I was told, although reluctantly so, and when my ear was inches away from his quivering mouth, my father whispered to me that my mother was a whore.

He actually used the word *prostitute*.

I moved back slightly to look at my father, wanting to know more. With even more struggle, and unforgettable pain displayed on his face, he whispered to me, "She had to go."

"What'd you mean?" I asked. "Where'd she go?"

My father took three rapid gasps, sounding like he wanted to explain himself but was battling some demon in his chest. Then he expired.

I never learned anything else about my mother, other than she was a whore. Whatever the full story was; it died with my father.

I returned to my studies following my father's burial. The School of Clinical Medicine of Cambridge. I was by far one of the most dedicated students.

That is an understatement.

But it is not a boast.

I am presenting who I was (and still am!) not only as a person but also in terms of how dedicated I was (and still am!) to my trade. To my goals.

At the university, even though I was still young, I felt that I was destined to tackle life's most difficult subjects. I felt that, no matter how long it would take, I would uncover some of the most revealing and magnificent details concerning the human mind. And today I can write that I have done just that, despite what the judge and those damn news outlets have said about me.

How can they be so wrong about me?

I don't know.

Perhaps I am too much of an individual.

It's always been that way.

At Cambridge, I was never one to hang around others. It's not that I find people disgusting. I find them very fascinating. This is why I wound up devoting so much time to understanding the human mind. But when it came to anything unrelated to my research, I never found the need to speak with others.

I was a loner.

I would only interact with those in my various study groups whenever essential. And I would of course converse with my suitemate, although I never had the same one for too long.

I had six different suitemates throughout my years at Cambridge. After a while, for reasons unknown to me, my suitemate would request a move and the university would provide me with another. But following the sixth departure, the university ceased with the substitutions and gave me the place to myself. I suppose all the switching was too much trouble for them.

I'm uncertain of why they all left. I don't believe I was rude or despicable. Perhaps it had something to do with my research.

In my early days, part of my independent research involved monitoring people while they slept. On occasion, a suitemate would wake up to me pointing a flashlight in their face as I feverously scribbled in my notebook. But I never thought I was crossing the line.

Who knows?

Perhaps the suitemates did not enjoy waking up to that type of surprise. Although if they ever stuck around long enough I'm certain at least one of them would've grown to appreciate my commitment.

NOTE #2

KAREN: *You mention commitment, and I understand what you're saying. But, to look at everything from another angle, do you think your past behavior could've possibly been attributable to obsession?*

DR. RAVENSDALE: *What's the difference?*

KAREN: *Well, having a solid commitment to something can be positive, especially in an occupational situation. But being obsessed can lead to isolation and destructiveness.*

DR. RAVENSDALE: *What's negative about isolation and destructiveness?*

No one stuck around in those days. I spent a lot of time by myself. It was for the best. With no friends I never felt obligated to attend social gatherings. This provided additional time to study.

I didn't have a girlfriend. In fact, I have never been lovingly, or even just sexually, touched. This too provided more time for my studies.

I didn't mind the isolation. Without distractions I was able to focus and carve out a proper route with my medical research.

One might argue that I did so because I felt left out. On the contrary. I stayed to myself and I studied the way I studied because one can learn many things while watching people from a distance.

I was always learning and it showed.

I was top of my class and received my degree with no issues. And then, in one of the proudest moments of my life, I eventually earned a job at Mount Sinai Hospital in New York City. It had always been a dream of mine to move to Manhattan and study a completely different breed of people.

The year was 1985 when I did just that.

Once I earned my stripes and became the go-to doctor at Mount Sinai, my colleagues began referring to me as "Mr. Precision." Not the finest of monikers. But I supposed it is one I understand.

I was known for my untiring passion and my unlimited ability to eliminate nearly all of my patient's ailments. For twenty-two years I walked the halls of that hospital like a treasured king. It felt great to be respected in that fashion. It felt even better to love with what I did.

I adored my profession. During those two decades, there was no other place I wanted to be other than that hospital. And can you guess how many lives I lost during those years? Can you guess how many people I was unable to keep alive? Twelve. That is all. In twenty-two years I lost only twelve lives! Those numbers are astonishing.

Think about those statistics. I treated thousands of patients, many of them on the verge of death, yet I only lost twelve. Think about how many people I saved!

I think about it all the time. I think about all those individuals I helped and it makes me laugh. I think about all the sperm I donated and the lives I might've created and it makes me lose it. Bloody hell.

What a man I was!

All of those saved lives yet here I am, confined and categorized as a lunatic. I've seen the reports. The guards have showed me the papers. Those bastards always show them in a disrespectful manner. They want me riled up! They want me to know what "The World" thinks of me.

Their attempts to anger me are ineffective! HA! What *The World* thinks of me! Whose world? Certainly not mine. I cannot relate to those who do not possess my skills. Those who do not have the intellectual capacity for my mission. I do not belong in *their* world. Nor them in mine!

As my time went on at the hospital, I was also able to become acquainted with a couple of younger doctors. These two would ultimately become my colleagues for my own personal research. For what would become my great experiment.

There are three reasons I wouldn't call these people friends. 1) As I've already made clear, I'm not one for friendship. 2) They were merely work associates for my important mission. 3) They turned out to be assholes.

I'm a realist, so I recognize that I initially needed these individuals, even though they eventually got in the way and one of them is even responsible for me being in this cell. Part of me still wants nothing but the worst for the one who helped put me here. But another part of me is still aware of the promise both of them once had. It was that promise that pushed me to bring them in on my experiment.

I'm still tremendously upset with them. Too upset to write their names. So I'll simply call them #1 and #2. It's easier this way since they were essentially two peas in a pod. A two-headed beast, if you will.

They both began working at the hospital approximately twelve years after my first day. Both of them were men. Both young and receptive. Most importantly, as our time at the hospital went on, both of them became captivated by me and my objectives.

With their talent, and my need for helping hands, and with the outstanding financial enticement I provided them, thanks in part to my own salary, as well as the large inheritance I received and invested after my father's death, I persuaded both #1 and #2 to leave the hospital to join my independent venture. To join one of the world's most significant examinations.

They quickly said yes.

III – The Details of My Experiment

All I ever wanted was to better appreciate the human mind. The brain is perhaps the most complex structure in the known universe, so I knew the task would be far from stress-free. But I was up to the challenge. I felt there was no one better than myself to analyze and expose why humans behave the way they do, particularly in relation to technology.

Following year upon year of examining our own goals and discovering how to tackle the research, my team concluded that we required a blank slate.

We had to be the team that dug the deepest.

Everyone has a theory for why those in the modern world are the way they are. Everyone has notions concerning why those who make up society are simultaneously different yet similar to those who roamed our land centuries ago. But not one person or controlled group has any concrete data.

I've read the published works of others, but it is mostly preposterous gibberish. Nothing more than hypothesis, in my opinion. I wanted to change that. I wanted to revolutionize the way we look at the brain.

I believe I succeeded in many ways.

Again, the first step was finding a blank slate. A blank slate with normal functions of course. The last thing we needed was for The Subject to develop and reveal some form of impairment. It would've created nothing more than wasted time. And if there is one thing I hate it is wasted time.

My team and I had to do our due diligence to acquire our clean slate. We had to bear down and investigate orphanages. Kidnapping a baby, although in the long run would've been easier and involved less paperwork, would've been unethical.

That's what #1 and #2 said.

The word *unethical* never crossed my mind. When it came to my experiment I never worried if something was considered "wrong."

There is no such thing as unethical when discovering earth-shattering information. I suppose what I was really considering back then was the word *unlawful*. The last thing I needed was the police ruining everything before I got my experiment off the ground. So the orphanage was essential.

Although money wasn't an issue, I still wanted this part of my experiment on the low side.

I sent #1 into the Tots and Treasures Orphanage to locate the best abandoned infant for the cheapest price.

Although I now despise him, #1 was quite the diligent worker at first. That meticulousness paid off. He took several trips to the facility and returned with forty-seven pages of notes summarizing his top five selections.

I pored over #1's notes to figure out the best candidate. One might imagine that infants are fairly similar. But one would be wrong.

Any infant with a birth defect didn't make it into the notes. There was no need for The Subject to have one arm or an addiction to crack. I'd go as far as to say that no one in this world needs anything like that.

There were also other factors at play.

Brain function was obviously a major one. Ethnicity was also high on the list. We needed a baby that would not be targeted or blocked in any situation.

I brought the top five down to two by eliminating from the running any infant that wasn't Caucasian.

Upon further review of #1's notes, I discovered that one of the two remaining infants cried more than the other. A tendency that would've been not only annoying, but also one that exhibited unacceptable feebleness. Although it turned out that I had to deal with a lot of crying anyway.

That was that. The decision had been made, by me of course, and the proper steps were taken for #1 to purchase The Subject.

NOTE #3

KAREN: *Didn't you or your colleagues feel at any moment that you were exploiting a human being?*

DR. RAVENSDALE: *Never. Not me, at least. People tend to think too much about the emotions of others. There's no need for that. People only comprehend the world they see. For The Subject, his entire world involved my experiment. He knew nothing else. As for my colleagues, they did protest a little, but they were too in awe of me at that point to go against my plans.*

Once The Subject was acquired, the next step for my team was to get a place we could call our live-in laboratory. We couldn't use the hospital for this type of work. There would've been too many hypercritical eyes. Plus, once our research heated up, we all had to resign and leave the hospital anyway. The workload became too much for us to stay at Mount Sinai.

I was happy to leave.

It's not that I didn't love my work there. I certainly did. But once I hit about year twenty-one I became fatigued and I yearned for new challenges. And that's exactly what my experiment would be: a new challenge.

So yes, we needed a location that would host my experiment. It didn't need to be extravagant. Us doctors had been dealing with bells and whistles for so many years that we learned what was truly essential. We required simplicity.

We eventually found and purchased a four bedroom home in Alabama, New York. The place was ideal. There weren't any other homes for at least another mile or two. That type of isolation was crucial. We didn't need meddlesome neighbors poking in and compromising my research.

Along with the four bedrooms, three of which would be used by #1, #2 and myself, the fourth used as my private study, there was also a large basement. This area I found most sensational.

The basement was *The World*. The basement is where almost everything of importance occurred. It is where me and my team raised The Subject and conducted most of our tests.

That's what this whole thing was about. The tests! My experiment wasn't about what all of the newspapers have stated. It wasn't about "mental torture" or "cult-like behavior" or "manipulating a human robot to murder and wreak havoc." No!

It wasn't about anything of that nature.

The fact that these journalists thought so shows me the truth. It shows me that they were nothing more than prattling muttonheads who could do nothing but misconstrue my work and write rubbish just to sell *their* stories. They were wrong. They were selling bullshit!

All I wanted, and worked so hard to accomplish, was to see what would happen to a person who was raised on virtually nothing but technology, all while having very little human contact.

This was one of the most important examinations in all of mankind. And when it came to carrying out such an important examination, I truly feel I succeeded on many levels.

It was by no means an easy task. Extraordinary devotion on my behalf was imperative. That and the proper arrangement. That's why the basement was perfect.

The basement was its own little home within our home. It had the essential items to keep The Subject alive. It had a crib which was later switched for a bed when The Subject matured. It also had a bucket for him to go to the bathroom once he was properly trained. On top of that, and more to the point of our experiment, the basement contained a desktop computer, a tablet computer, and later on it even had a television. It was a must for the Subject to be constantly stimulated by technology.

There were no books or literary magazines. That would've been too risky. Studies have shown that fiction is good for the mind, particularly when it comes to the imagination. We didn't need that for this experiment. We needed an obedient soldier. One that would follow my lead no matter the demand.

When The Subject was old enough to read — a skill I personally taught him — it was only material from websites I allowed him to view. That material was occasionally linked to pornographic websites. There is a reason for that. We'll arrive at that point later.

All was set.

We had time to work since leaving the hospital. We had the finances thanks to myself and my inheritance. We had the location where most of our work would be conducted. Most importantly, we had The Subject.

For all that's been said and done, I must say how pleased I am with how things turned out with The Subject. Not everything. But most things.

I realize this is odd of me to say since I'm currently incarcerated with no hope of being released. But I can't hide the fact that I am pretty damn satisfied with the results.

There are different variables that come into play regarding the human mind. There are very few certainties. You can have ideas and intricately designed strategies, but they could all go out the window if your subject has some undetected defect. A mental deficiency of some sort. Even something like a panic disorder can derail the subject and devastate the research.

No matter the detail put into our background check, there was still the possibility of The Subject being useless.

This fortunately did not occur.

The early years of my research weren't overly demanding. As an infant, and eventually as a toddler, The Subject was easy to manage. All I had to do was feed him and change him and make sure he didn't die.

He never cried all that much when he was that young. An additional benefit. When he did cry, me and my team would simply focus on our work and let our studies drown out the sound. Soon enough his infrequent bawling became nothing more than unobtrusive noise.

There were moments here and there when we forgot to change his diaper after he soiled himself. There were times where he would sit in his own waste for a few days. But none of us were there to be fathers. We were men of science. Forget affection. We were there to use our wits and conduct the experiment without becoming attached.

With that said, I feel we did a fine job keeping The Subject alive and healthy during the early years. Even if that wasn't the point.

So what was the point?

The point was simple yet innovative.

Me and my two former colleagues would be the first team ever to raise a human being almost entirely by use of technology.

When The Subject became old enough for proper development, we programmed several alphabet tutoring and word association videos for the child to watch. We did this day after day.

As the years went on, the videos became more enhanced and wide-ranging. Even if the topic was mundane, we made sure The Subject understood every element. We showed him everything from the right way to cut one's food, to the way to dress oneself. We showed him videos on working out. We even showed him a tutorial on how to proficiently masturbate.

To make sure we didn't create cerebral disproportionateness, not wanting The Subject to have issues with communication, I had #2, a highly skilled robotic engineer, build a machine that conversed with The Subject. Nothing too long or drawn out, of course. Merely a back and forth that would introduce The Subject to what it's like to exchange.

This exercise turned out to be unsuccessful. I wound up scrapping #2's machine. But our intentions were good.

The training sessions went on for years. Unlike anything else I've participated in or spearheaded in my life, each day was better than the last. There were certainly moments when The Subject would experience some sort of setback. But I always felt prepared for such instances.

When The Subject was thirteen there were occasions where he would weep in an overpowering manner. Sometimes for hours on end. He would also occasionally self-harm. Unprovoked, he would bash his head against the hard stone wall of the basement.

But I was never overly concerned. I was a professional. And I was an optimist. I always viewed the self-harming behavior as a bonus. It was as if I was breaking down The Subject's mental walls and seeing his genuine outlook on life.

In his chaos I witnessed beauty.

Those early moments showed me that I was bound to get somewhere with this experiment. I was getting to the TRUTH! Yes! I felt that no one would be able to dispute this.

My only complaint is that I wish I had more time to study. But that would not be so.

***

My experiment concluded on The Subject's eighteenth birthday. I would've loved to continue for many years. I could've seen it proceeding until I arrived at my deathbed. Not with him, of course. With another. But no. The goddamn police put an end to it.

Well, I can't fully blame the police. I had to partially put an end to the experiment in my own way. Or at least put an end to the course that it was on. Secondly, back to the police, I can't blame them in an occupational sense. They were doing their jobs. They had been appointed to carry out their work in accordance to the rules of society. It just so happens that these guidelines are bullshit.

So I suppose I am blaming society.

Yes.

I blame society for their inability to see the bigger picture. I blame them for not providing me the time to figure out other avenues with my experiment.

That is my biggest complaint. Being unfairly judged doesn't worry me much. Not being able to use my arms, or even go to the bathroom without help, I can handle that. But knowing that I still have so much more to learn yet no way of attaining that education, that's the hardest pill to swallow.

But all in all, I have still accomplished a great amount. More than others could, can, or will ever have the balls to imagine.

The only thing left for me to do is detail the greater accomplishments of my experiment.

I'll tell you again to disregard what the news outlets have said about me. What you are about to read is the outright reality.

It wasn't always easy. It wasn't always clean. If one is using their mind only in relation to the rules of society, as opposed to a mind linked with science, it wasn't always legal. But forget that. Worrying about absurd laws would've tampered with my brain.

Fortunately, I did not let that happen.

And fortunately, no matter how many pills this institution forces into my system, I can still provide the details of my experiment. The experiment that has in many ways changed the world, and will continue to do so for generations to come.

I will now show you how I made a brand new type of person.

Test #1 – The Job

Whether it happens early in their life or at some point down the road, the importance of professional work becomes very clear to a human being. There are many different elements to consider when it comes to an occupation. There are some who realize the essentialness of not only making a living but also of finding a career early on in their lives. Then there are those who don't know, or perhaps don't care, to consider a career during their youth.

Those in the latter category usually go on to struggle at deadbeat job after deadbeat job, only to hate themselves and everyone else around them, all the while barely making enough money to breath and sleep. That type of existence is never desirable. An obvious understatement. Yet one I feel isn't mentioned enough.

Times have unquestionably changed since I was a young lad in England. It's odd. I feel it was more difficult to succeed back then, even though there were more opportunities in those days, at least in my circle.

Although there seems to be fewer prospects these days, there are certainly more ways to find work. There are easier and faster methods to send materials out for consideration. With the ability to send e-mails, the act of heading door to door for work has all but evaporated. There are now a number of websites dedicated to helping someone find work. Opportuneness at its finest.

There are indeed advantages to this.

As well as disadvantages.

For the run of the mill worker, there are no longer a plethora of jobs to choose from. Yet, one would imagine that thanks to technology the ability to put oneself out there has risen.

I found this scenario very fascinating. I couldn't stop pondering if this convenience was actually counterproductive. I couldn't help but to wonder if the easy access was more damaging than accommodating for an applicant's mindset.

I might be alone with this thought, but I do not believe that clicking on a computer and sending out through e-mail builds the proper character traits one requires to land a job. I believe being face to face with another only helps. Particularly if one is face to face with a hiring manager. There is such a thing called spontaneity, and one never knows what positive statement might emerge during a conversation.

On paper, or a Word Document, one can be at the same level as another applicant. But during an interview one can say something that stands out and get the job because of that statement.

I've been in meetings before where things weren't going my way, but due to me being in the room, I was able to read the situation, adjust my approach, and attain exactly what I wanted.

There are of course exceptions to this. Like when I was in the interrogation room with those detectives. Nothing I said had the power to sway them. But I don't think that was my fault. They already had their minds made up.

Despite that nonsense, I'm still a firm advocate for the face to face approach. I believe in the advantages it presents.

But I still wasn't convinced. I wasn't sure if I was correct or if I was being skeptical about the technological world. This is why I conducted Test #1. I knew my team and I would be able to utilize The Subject and discover concrete answers on this matter.

The first step was getting The Subject to an age where he could work an actual job. Obviously we had to keep him alive to get to that point. We did so by feeding him whenever necessary and injecting him with Butorphanol to induce sleep and then a Pentedrone injection to wake him in the mornings and provide energy. It was a must to keep The Subject on a proper routine. A schedule that would work best for us doctors. This way we could control the experiment.

Once The Subject was old enough to comprehend the working world, my team provided him with occupational information, all the while trying to figure out if he had any particular skillset.

He did not.

We showed him online videos of wage-earning workers performing and explaining their trades. We showed The Subject videos of electricians installing electrical wiring. Videos of landscapers gardening various yards. We even showed him videos of ironworkers erecting the steel framework of buildings.

The Subject was bored while these videos played. No. Not even bored. It was actually as if he was in pain watching the footage. It was as if he wanted nothing to do with the lessons.

The Subject would fidget and sigh after only thirty seconds of us putting on a video. He would occasionally try to escape from his chair, but these attempts were pointless since I would hold him down.

There were occasions where The Subject was so bored he would close his eyes as tightly as possible, hoping this would make the tediousness go away. I did my best to prevent this.

Following the first time, I made sure to hold his eyelids open for every video session. A pain in the ass maneuver. It sometimes worked. Sometimes not so much. It all depended on how much The Subject squirmed.

This all might sound harsh but, believe me, it was absolutely necessary. I had an experiment to conduct.

***

Although The Subject showed no interest in the videos, I still believed some information possibly penetrated his barricade. Wanting to see if that happened, I set up a rudimentary worksite in the corner of the basement. Well, I wouldn't call it a worksite. It was merely a section dedicated to a physical task.

Once I brought them in from outside, I set up thirteen rocks, all varying in size, but one never exceeding twenty-five pounds, and set them in the basement. After screaming in The Subject's face like a drill sergeant for exactly ten minutes, I then commanded him to move the rocks from the pile to a red x I marked on the floor. The red x was only five feet away from the pile. I figured this simple task was enough to grasp The Subject's abilities.

It was.

It didn't matter to me whether or not The Subject did well. All that mattered was that I saw a result. And what a result it was.

I got to see the incredible laziness of The Subject. When commanded to begin his task, The Subject emitted a drawn-out groan, exhibiting how badly he wanted nothing to do with the heavy lifting, and shoved his hands deep inside the pockets of his only pair of jeans.

He continued to whine until I grabbed him by his cheeks and told him once more to move the rocks, this time with a little more bass in my voice. The Subject was visibly upset, and he did release a powerful grunt, but he complied nonetheless.

Somewhat.

The Subject's entire body trembled after moving the first rock. This reaction was caused by a mixture of irritation and exhaustion. After moving the second rock, almost dropping it on his foot, either from being too drained or too sluggish to place it down gently, The Subject began weeping.

The cries were excessive. Not just a single tear or a lone sniffle. The Subject cried as if he just witnessed the slaughter of his parents. That couldn't be true, of course. He didn't know his parents. If anything, I was the closest thing he had to a parent.

On and on he cried, occasionally snorting and mumbling to himself. I had witnessed all I needed. I was happy with the results. I was prepared to move on to the next step.

Taking back control, I smacked The Subject across the face seven times. This shut him up.

The Subject needed to know that I was the one at the helm. That I was the one setting the tone and choosing the time and place for the presentation of his feelings.

He was bound to learn quickly, whether he wanted to or not.

NOTE #4

KAREN: *Don't you feel that violence worked against you in the long run? Don't you think The Subject felt more terrified than motivated and thus unable to fully develop his mental aptitude?*

DR. RAVENSDALE: *That's a fair question. But no, I don't believe that to be the case. I used to toe the line and never ruffle any feathers. There was a time when I never even raised my voice. And sure, my life was just fine during that period, but it was never astonishing. It wasn't until I became forceful that I started to see just how rousing I could be, and how I could turn a normal existence into an extraordinary one.*

Following the rock portion of Test #1, me and my team still had to keep moving forward at a fast pace. It's never a good thing to let your foot off the gas.

Once we understood The Subject's work ethic, we created a list of places where he might be able to work.

It was a very short list.

That short list was filed down to one place and one place only. This was all on account of #2 having a connection at a library roughly an hour away from the laboratory.

#2 called in a favor with his friend who managed the library and got The Subject a position as an assistant. Great news for us. But we kept our celebrations discreet. We didn't want The Subject to know about his job at first.

All we let The Subject believe was that it was now time for him to reach out to various companies in order to find a job. It may seem like a waste of time, given that he was officially hired at the library, but this was a crucial part of my test.

I had The Subject create a Word Document detailing information about himself. Information regarding abilities and desires. This was something I had to help him with since he didn't fully know who he was. Then I had The Subject write an e-mail that would be, "sent out to several hiring agents."

Even though he could read and write, creating this e-mail took a while. The Subject utilized atrocious sentence fragments, misspelt more than a few words, and frequently used acronyms to make the process easier on himself.

This type of email would not stand. I wouldn't tolerate such a display of idiocy. I made The Subject write his messages over and over until they were correct and professional. This process was far from simple.

Every time he had to reread and rewrite his message The Subject would whimper and flail his arms like a disobedient preschooler. I would let him go on for a bit. That is until I felt it was time to get back to work. Then I would snap him back into play him with my electroshock weapon. That's right. I would shock him with the stun gun I purchased specifically for my experiment.

Using my stun gun always silenced The Subject. That is of course after his pain from the shock finally abated.

He would get back to work once that happened.

The best part is that none of the messages written by The Subject actually mattered. They were all being sent to various email accounts that I created.

What I would do next is act like the hiring managers and send rejections back to The Subject. I would be extremely punitive and unsympathetic in these rejections. I frequently criticized The Subject's intellect. In fact, #2 said on one occasion that I was, "going for the throat."

He made this statement almost in condemning fashion. I didn't like his tone. I was in charge of the experiment. Not him. I informed #2 that if he questioned me again it would be *his* throat I'd go after. Just like The Subject after being stunned, #2 quieted down as well.

I knew what I was doing.

I was testing to see how far I could push The Subject. I was testing to see how well he could handle rejection. And let me tell you; he did not handle it well.

It was clear from the first two rejections that The Subject was confounded by what was taking place. He couldn't grasp the reason for the denial. He felt that since he had sent the message he was guaranteed a position.

When he received the third rejection, The Subject threw his hands in the air as if to say, "This is pointless," and started growling at his laptop.

I told him that type of mentality would not be permitted.

I then banned him from the internet that night by removing his devices from the basement. That entire evening I heard him howling and slamming his head against the stone wall.

The following day, once I stitched and bandaged the wound on his forehead, I returned his internet privileges. I was happy to do so since waiting in his inbox was rejection #4.

The Subject was hesitant to open the message. The look on his face said, "It's not worth it. I've already been through enough torture."

Torture? You don't know what torture is, son! That's what I was thinking as I looked at his expression.

But I maintained reasonableness. I did not shout. I calmly told The Subject that he had had no other choice but to open the message. I told him it was important. I informed him of the significance of becoming employed. I told him that he would be considered pathetic in my eyes if he didn't open the message and get a job.

After some more fidgeting and indecision, The Subject finally opened the message. His face dropped as he read the words of rejection.

As soon as he finished reading, just to make sure the words fully sunk in, I stood over his shoulder and recited the message out loud. I wanted him to hear the words from someone else. I wanted him to hear the reasons he wasn't good enough.

The Subject didn't take this too well. He pulled large clumps of hair from his scalp during my reading.

An interesting reaction.

I once again removed his devices from the basement and left him down there alone to scream.

"Agh! Agh! Agh! Agh!" The Subject shouted this grating noise for hours and hours and hours until suddenly all went silent.

I wasn't watching my video monitors showing the feed of the basement. I was upstairs relaxing in my office when the sounds abruptly terminated. I just figured The Subject simply became tired and fell asleep. That was partially true.

The next morning, I unlocked the basement door and went down to inspect The Subject. I found him lying in somewhat of a pool of his own blood. Most of the blood had already dried on the basement floor, so it wasn't a complete pool. I patched him up once again and brought him back around with a shot of Pentedrone.

From all of this I was able to make a clear evaluation: The Subject did not at all enjoy, understand, or learn from rejection.

I saw the reason for The Subject's latest laceration when I went back to watch the video from the night before. After I left the basement, while he screamed and rushed around like a lunatic, The Subject powerfully brought his head down on the edge of his desk. It was a vicious blow. Blood sprayed like a slightly gripped garden hose.

It was hard for me to tell whether or not this maneuver was accidental or something The Subject did deliberately to knock himself out.

***

The time had come for positive news.

Following an exasperating amount of convincing, given that he was scared to receive another rejection, after I once again brandished my stun gun, The Subject opened his fifth e-mail and read that he had landed a job.

This message was official given that it came from #2's connection.

The message stated that The Subject's application was well-received and that work would begin the following Monday. I remember it all very clearly. That message arrived on a Thursday morning. This provided me and my team four days to prepare The Subject.

The key was to not have any negative influence on the experiment. We didn't want to do anything that might get in the way of the internet's lessons. But there were certain things we could do to make sure he at least looked the part.

A bath followed by a haircut and a shave was certainly in order. It had been several months at that point since The Subject had been scrubbed and groomed. He was beginning to resemble a repulsive animal.

Once he was clean and presentable, I arranged a sleeping schedule that would connect with working hours.

Four days was just enough time for me to craft and inject the proper blend of medication. Injections that would have The Subject falling asleep by 10pm and rising at 6am.

One would imagine it would be enough to merely tell The Subject to sleep. But that was not the case. He was very attached to his own schedule. The Subject's main hours of operation were opposite to what is considered normal. He would get lost searching the internet until about four or five in the morning. This would not have been good for his job.

The thought crossed my mind to once again revoke his internet privileges, but that might've caused more harm than good. The Subject had developed a temper, particularly when it came to his time online, so if I had removed his devices yet again he would've just stayed up all night damaging himself.

Not only would we have had a fatigued Subject working at the library, we also would have had one twice as disfigured and bandaged.

Injecting him some more was the best course of action.

The final phase with our prep work, and arguably the most vital step, involved setting up cameras in the library. In the eyes of The Library Manager, he was just helping a friend by giving #2's "nephew" a job. The Library Manager had no idea about the experiment. We aimed to keep it that way.

I sent my colleagues to the library on the Saturday before The Subject's first day to orchestrate everything. #1 would be #2's "friend visiting from California". And while #2 struck up a conversation with The Library Manager #1 would saunter off and stealthily place small cameras around the library. This would enable us to keep an eye on The Subject without raising suspicion.

Everything came together nicely.

The only issue was The Subject's attitude. It was only a minor issue, especially since it helped me gain further understanding of his psyche, but it was a problem nonetheless. The issue was that, in his own way, The Subject started to complain a lot. The closer we got to his first day of work the more he grumbled.

It began with him vigorously shaking his head while belting out loud grunts. It then escalated to him sobbing and violently smacking his own face with both hands. He would occasionally look like an irate ape pounding his own features. He was obviously uncomfortable with the job. He felt like he had already been through enough by trying to get the job. He felt like he had already worked as hard as possible. He clearly needed to vent out his frustration.

I would let him scream for a little while. I didn't mind it as long as it was within reason. For me to comprehend him, even though he wasn't using actual words, it was important for The Subject to express himself. But I would show him my stun gun when he went on for too long and I thought he might jeopardize the experiment. Worked like a charm.

It was getting to the point where I usually didn't have to use the device. Given that he had already felt the pain, he knew that silence was essential when the stun gun made an appearance.

That might be considered overly forceful. But when it came to pulling off this test, my forcefulness was necessary. And it was that

43

ability to be forceful that made me both the brain and the muscle of the experiment.

How'd you like that?

No one from my secondary school would've ever believed this would take place. Oh no. They would punch me and kick me and spit on me and urinate on me and never believe that I would become a man of strength. Well look at me now, you bastards! I became a dominant force! I became a man who could control another person without speaking a single word. How do you like that for power?

NOTE #5

KAREN: *Do you feel that being tormented when you were younger influenced your behavior with The Subject?*

DR. RAVENSDALE: *How'd you mean?*

KAREN: *Did you mistreat The Subject because you were beaten as an adolescent?*

DR. RAVENSDALE: *Mistreat?*

KAREN: *Well...*

DR. RAVENSDALE: *Stop it. Don't be daft. The Subject was nothing more than a small bolt in a big machine. Haven't you ever yelled at your remote control or any of your electronic devices when they weren't working properly?*

The morning of The Subject's first workday arrived and my team couldn't have been more thrilled. We had been doing other tests up to that point, but it felt as if those tests led up to this moment. Years in the making!

We had done the necessary work and felt prepared. We knew all the nuts and bolts of The Subject. This provided us with the feeling of readiness and the willingness to accept whatever might happen at the library. His very first job.

It also happened to be The Subject's last job. But that was okay. What eventually took place not only provided a result but also the reality of The Subject's mindset.

Thanks to my methodical method of injecting The Subject, he was awake that Monday nice and early at 6am. He looked fresh. Clear-eyed. But not wanting to risk the chance of him crashing later on, I doubled his dose of morning Pentedrone. I wanted…no…I *needed* him to be on top of his game. I needed to see how someone with his psychosomatic background could handle the working world. I needed to see this without him walking around like a zombie.

After his injection, I fixed him breakfast and laid out his clothes. When he held up his tie, motioning to me that he needed help, I scoffed and said, "That is not why I am here."

I told him to take advantage of the device he'd been using most of his life. Then I left him to it, making sure to slam shut the basement door for added emphasis.

Once upstairs I made my way over to the video monitor and watched the action. The Subject held the tie in his hands and, with confused eyes, stared at it for two minutes and forty-seven seconds. He then paced around the basement snarling to himself for one minute and twenty-nine seconds.

He brought his frantic strides to an end and went to his laptop, finally understanding this to be the place where he would find a video on tying a proper knot. He discovered a video he could comprehend. He watched that five-minute video three times in a row. After the third play The Subject began bawling. This crying episode lasted three minutes and forty-nine seconds.

When he realized that no one was coming to help, The Subject calmed himself to watch the video again and actually took a shot with his tie. Nine attempts later, following more weeping, he finally figured it out. It wasn't the perfect tie. But it would do.

The Subject was starting to learn how to handle things himself.

It was slightly difficult to get The Subject moving once he was wearing his tie. As soon as his knot was secure he sat down in front of his laptop and began reading the comments on the video's page. He read intently. He read slowly and with no emotion on his face. He didn't seem to get any actual enjoyment out of the process. It was almost as if he felt obligated to read the comments and, due to this requirement, did so in robotic fashion.

I got The Subject moving by playing the tie video on his tablet and moving with the device toward the exit of the basement. Enticement. He pursued like a ravenous dog following a treat all the way to my van/mobile laboratory.

Once inside the vehicle, The Subject's eyes didn't leave the tablet throughout the entire ride. He read the comments on one page and then clicked on other pages to read the comments displayed there. With no visible joy or frustration, The Subject was consumed by the comments of strangers until we arrived at the library.

Getting him out of my van was all the more difficult. Given that he was about to enter a place of business, I did not allow him to bring the tablet. He didn't understand. He made faces as if I was punishing him. When I wouldn't concede he slammed his head against the back of the passenger seat. It was cushion so his wounds didn't reopen.

I flashed my stun gun.

This brought him back to a level of steadiness.

I attached to The Subject's ankle a GPS tracking device that I purchased online. This way he wouldn't get far if he tried to run away.

#2 grabbed The Subject's arm and aggressively removed him from the van, taking him inside the library to begin his first day of work.

With The Subject out of the mobile laboratory, #1 and I set up the video monitors for our surveillance. We waited for The Subject to exit the vehicle since we didn't want the sight of equipment to be disconcerting.

I never knew if The Subject was aware that he was being recorded almost continuously. I wasn't sure if he'd react negatively to that information. So I figured the experiment would be better off without him knowing that little detail.

#2 entered the library with The Subject and, following some polite dialogue with his friend, rushed back to the mobile laboratory. The thing most immediately noticeable was the uncomfortable nature of The Subject. This was obvious even before #2 left the library.

After he said farewell and moved toward the exit, The Subject latched onto #2's arm like a terrified adolescent. I found this behavior most displeasing. It reminded me of a father/son bond. I felt that I was the only one who had built that type of relationship with The Subject.

I gave #2 a severe dressing-down when he returned to the mobile laboratory. I told him to keep things professional and informed him that it wasn't his job to become emotionally close to The Subject. He tried claiming that he wasn't doing such a thing. I didn't like his tone so I viciously clapped my hands in front of his face to create silence.

It worked.

Another person who was dissatisfied by The Subject's actions was The Library Manager, although for different reasons altogether. The Subject's abnormal conduct was highly immature. Perhaps even a touch psychotic.

Given his age, seeing that The Subject was in his late teens, it was certainly odd to see him on the verge of tears as he clawed at #2. Luckily, The Library Manager simply considered it an unusual case of first day nerves and didn't let the behavior get in the way.

My team watched from the mobile laboratory as The Library Manager walked around with The Subject, telling him about his tasks. It should've been an easy job for The Subject. All he had to do was file a few titles every so often, reorganize the magazine and video racks whenever necessary, and assist anyone who had questions.

Yes, it should've been easy.

I suppose one could argue what eventually took place should've never happened. But I do not subscribe to that philosophy. I do not support the theory of *should've could've would've*.

With a test of this nature, it is vital for absolutely nothing to be off limits.

Anything that happened was supposed to happen for my experiment, as well as for the greater good of humanity.

***

While being led around the library, The Subject could not hide his discomposure. He couldn't stop scratching his neck. He was digging in like a desiccating fiend. His neck was raw before The Library Manager finally spoke up.

"Are you okay?" The Library Manager asked. "Do you have a rash or something? Something I may need to know about?"

The Subject said nothing. He stared at The Library Manager for six seconds before looking at the carpet below.

Doubt intensified within The Library Manager, but he carried on.

He knew he was doing a favor for #2, so he felt he must continue the tour.

Throughout most of the tour, The Subject's eyes would not stop darting toward the small cluster of computers set in the middle of the library. To The Subject this cluster was Shangri-La.

Taking notice of The Subject's attention, perhaps as a way to get rid of the weirdness, The Library Manager told him that he could use a computer: "Whenever we're slow and no patrons are using them."

The Library Manager went on to say, "I don't want you to be bored. But I also want you to uphold a certain level of professionalism here."

The Subject never made it to the end of that sentence.

By the time The Library Manager said the word *bored* The Subject sprinted off to one of the computers. He sat down and tried to search the internet. Not knowing he needed a password to log in, The Subject started banging on the keyboard and smacking the side of the monitor.

Shocked and panicked, The Library Manager ran over to The Subject and quickly provided him the login information. He walked away mumbling something about a "big mistake."

The beginning of the work day stayed on a stable course, at least for The Subject. There were things to do around the library, but, for the most part, The Subject remained seated at the computer searching the internet.

The Library Manager would walk past in a very deliberate manner, sometimes emitting a low puff of frustration or an exaggerated cough, trying to get The Subject's attention. As if a tactic so diplomatic could work.

It was clear that he wanted The Subject to do more than sit around. But it was also clear that The Library Manager wasn't a man who called the shots. He didn't feel comfortable bossing around The Subject.

But sometimes he didn't have a choice.

When work became too much for one man to handle, The Library Manager had to ask for help, which of course was his right. When this happened, The Subject would initially pretend to not hear

The Library Manager. But then, after much persistence from his boss, The Subject would finally give in by letting out a bad-mannered moan before lethargically rising from seat to do the job he was hired to perform.

It was quite interesting.

Never in my line of work had I ever seen such a self-opinionated character. I never tolerated such an attitude when I worked at the hospital. But that seemed to be another world. What I was witnessing during Test #1 was completely different. The Subject was acting as if The Library Manager was getting in *his* way.

And somehow The Library Manager kept a calm demeanor. I don't know how he did it. Perhaps on past occasions he had to deal with that type of entitlement and was accustomed to the attitude. Perhaps he thought that a composed response would be his best course of action.

It wasn't.

He would learn that soon enough.

The Library Manager continued with his composed method, even as he dragged The Subject around to perform miniscule tasks. When The Subject wasn't on the verge of tears, he would keep his eyes locked on the computer. His expression was one of pure desperation. He looked as if he was stranded in the blistering desert, so close to death, and only the computer could deliver hydration.

The Subject would angrily growl when a specific duty went on longer than a couple of minutes. He did this while looking at his feet, as if unsure of what to do with his fury. The Subject was too socially inept to hold eye contact with the one irritating him.

***

The closer the time moved toward 12:00PM, the more The Library Manager told The Subject about, "The lunch time rush."

He informed The Subject that it was best to grab a bite beforehand since it was bound to get busy, also dropping hints that The Subject wouldn't be able to use the computer from that point until around 2:00PM.

The Subject paid no attention to this. He continued searching the internet. The Library Manager shook his head and walked away, clearly regretting his decision to help #2.

12:00pm arrived.

Just as The Library Manager projected, loads of people entered the establishment. At first, The Subject didn't seem concerned with the activity. It actually seemed as if he didn't notice it. He was too involved with his device.

But the number of patrons continued to grow. Many perused the library's books. Some just congregated to chat or participate in study groups. And then there were those who were using the computers. One by one, the computers around The Subject became occupied, all until the only not being used by a patron was the one being used by the employee.

An older woman stood behind The Subject patiently waiting her turn. She had no idea he was an employee of the library. Why would she? He displayed no signs of it.

After waiting for what seemed to be far too long, in an attempt to get his attention, the older woman finally tapped The Subject on the shoulder. He took no notice of this initial tap. He was mentally lost on a website showing *urban street fights*, reading and softly grunting at the comments at the bottom of the page.

The Older Woman tapped again.

The second tap caught The Subject's attention.

The Library Manager happened to glance up at this moment and saw what was taking place. Whether it was a case of bad timing is not for me to say. What I can say is that when The Older Woman tapped the second time The Subject looked over his shoulder slowly, almost like an alarmed beast, and started growling once again. But these growls were louder. More malicious than the earlier ones.

The Library Manager dashed over to settle things. It was clear that The Older Woman was shaken. But The Library Manager quickly diffused the situation by yanking The Subject away from the computer and politely inviting The Older Woman to sit.

Although tentative at first, The Older Woman ultimately agreed and sat down in front of the computer. In front of The Subject's sacred instrument. Once she was settled, The Older Woman decided not to complain about The Subject's actions. This was not only fortunate for the experiment, since I'm sure any grievance would've led to The Library Manager firing The Subject, but surprising as well, given his gross misconduct.

Perhaps The Older Woman was a very tolerant person. Or perhaps she thought The Subject was mentally challenged and felt bad for him. I don't know. It's not for me to say.

What I can say is that she should've left the library. She should've gotten out of there before it all went down.

I'd even go as far as to say she was partially to blame for everything.

***

The Library Manager reprimanded The Subject as he pulled him away from the computer. I was surprised he had that type of power in him. Frustrated, out of his comfort zone, The Library Manager used the type of whisper that's decidedly livid. Like when a mother yells at her children in church for mucking about.

"What is wrong with you?" The Library Manager asked The Subject. "Honestly. Please tell me what I'm dealing with here."

The Library Manager might not have had the backbone to fire The Subject, but I was certain he would later call #2 and tell him to not return with his "nephew."

What a specimen The Subject was turning out to be.

He couldn't even hold down the simplest of jobs. He couldn't even keep a job where most of the work was done *for* him. And you know what; this was fine by me and my team. It was a result. We learned what we set out to learn. We learned that when it came to the working world, The Subject's lifestyle had turned him into an inert, self-important little creature with no respect for others.

All that was left for us to do was let The Subject close out the day and bring an end to Test #1.

My team sat back in the mobile laboratory and relaxed a bit, feeling as if the rest of the day would be mostly the same. But then, something caught my eye.

The Library Manager was keeping a tight leash on The Subject, so to speak. After his growling episode, The Library Manager had The Subject stand next to him at the front desk as he went through some files. This was making The Subject rather antsy.

It was the stressed twitching of The Subject's right leg that first caught my eye. My attention was pulled in even more when the recurring spasm of his left shoulder began. Suddenly, The Subject was once again clawing at his already raw neck. His anxiety was intensifying. But The Library Manager didn't seem concerned, just as long as he kept The Subject close by.

The Subject's scratching became worse over time. It was as if he was attempting to dig to the center of his own throat.

More time went by. The lunchtime rush died down and people gradually exited the library. The Subject thought that with so few people he'd be able to return to a computer.

No go.

The Library Manager was through with his employee's unusual behavior and kept The Subject by his side.

I didn't agree with this tactic.

The only people left in library were The Library Manager, the older woman who took The Subject's computer, and The Subject. There was nothing to do in an occupational sense.

The Subject hadn't used a computer for two hours, three minutes and twenty-seven seconds, and, if anything, I think he might've earned the right to get back behind the screen.

But The Library Manager would not give in. I suppose he wanted to prove a point. #2 should've warned him against that.

What took place next happened in a flash.

Well, I supposed it had been one large build-up. But the act itself was just as swift as it was powerful. And it was *quite* powerful.

The Library Manager informed The Subject that the time had come to clean the mess created by the lunchtime rush. When The Subject didn't immediately comply, The Library Manager hostilely took hold of The Subject's wrist, planning to pull him toward the work.

Faster than the snap of a finger, The Subject grabbed The Library Manager's arm and twisted it violently until a loud crack rang out. The Subject had been watching hours of fight footage down in the basement during those months and had obviously learned some maneuvers.

The Library Manager howled and dropped to the floor like a squashed ragdoll. As he wailed and writhed in pain and called desperately for help, The Subject's focus zoomed over to The Older Woman. She sat at the computer frozen from fear. The breaking of The Library Manager's arm happened too quickly and skillfully for her to see it happen, but she definitely heard the thunderous screams.

As The Older Woman sat there stunned and terrified over the commotion, The Subject gave a rapid yet mighty kick to The Library

Manager's knee, shattering it and rendering the crushed man virtually immobile. He then leapt over the front desk like a wild animal and sprinted toward The Older Woman.

Falling to pieces, the only thing The Older Woman could squeak out was: "Oh, wait…I don't…"

No one heard what was coming after the word *don't*. Who knows if The Older Woman had anything coherent to say? How could she? She looked so petrified.

I couldn't blame her. The Subject charged after her like an incensed bull and didn't stop until he knocked her backward off the chair. A thud blared out as her body landed hard on the unforgiving floor.

The Older Woman had her hand on the computer monitor as The Subject knocked her over. She took the monitor down with her as she fell. The Subject let out a spine-tingling roar, fearing that device might break, but still moved quick enough catch the monitor before it crashed.

I had my records taken away from me following my arrest, but I do recall jotting down the note: Quick reaction speed.

The Subject viewed The Older Woman's actions as her not caring about the computer. This is something The Subject loathed. It pushed him over the edge.

The raging fire in his eyes was beyond evident. He wanted blood. He wanted revenge for having his internet taken away and his device nearly destroyed.

By the time The Older Woman tried to boost herself off the ground, The Subject was already in what I believe to be a karate stance and used his right foot, which was covered by a steel toe boot, to kick The Older Woman across her face. Her nose busted. Blood exploded all over her head neck and chest. She looked as if she had just been standing in between two colliding vehicles.

All that destruction with just one kick.

The Older Woman began sniveling and pleading for compassion. This did not register with The Subject. He looked at her with a puzzled expression, as if he was trying to grasp the human emotions she displayed.

"I don't know what I did," The Older Woman cried out. "Please…"

The Subject did not let The Older Woman finish her statement. He weighed her down by putting his knee on her chest and started wailing away. Unmercifully, The Subject threw punch after punch into The Older Woman's face. Her chin, cheeks, ears, eyes, her forehead. No area was safe from punishment. The Subject turned her features into nothing more than one mashed bloody lump. Then he went on punching some more.

Once The Older Woman's cries were no more and existence was agonizingly slipping away from her, it no longer sounded like The Subject was thrashing an actual human being. It sounded more like he was pummeling a timeworn bag of wet noodles.

But this didn't stop him.

He went on and on and on.

It seemed as if The Subject could've continued punching The Older Woman's face endlessly, even after he had finally beat the life out of her. And I'm pretty sure he would've done so if it wasn't for the noise across the room.

The sound of The Library Manager.

He had finally shaken off the shock he suffered from having his bones broken and was now standing on his one good leg. The look on his face was a concoction of pain, disgust and horror. I'm sure if he wasn't so scared for his life he would've retched all over the place. A man like that is never prepared for the inhumaneness of humanity.

The Library Manager gasped and did his best to hobble toward the exit. It was the gasp that alerted The Subject, breaking him away from his pummeling.

The Library Manager wanted nothing more than to save his own life. But The Subject was faster.

It was then that I realized that if The Subject wanted something he was sure as hell going to get it. He was pathetic during the rock exercise in the basement. His legitimate work in the library was doubly pitiful. But this was because he wanted nothing to do with either of the two. He saw no incentive for the hard work. But when it came to revenge against The Library Manager, it's safe to say that this was something he certainly wanted.

Want is putting it lightly.

He *craved* retribution for having his internet taken away.

The Library Manager made it a foot or two closer to the exit before he was grabbed and yanked to the floor by The Subject. He had his keys in his hand as if he would make it to the exit and lock in The Subject. Those keys went flying once he was caught.

The Subject grabbed The Library Manager by his good arm and broke that one as well. Perhaps for good measure.

The snap rang out as did the new cries of The Library Manager. The terrible cries of pain. The cries for mercy. The cries for God's help.

#2 finally had enough. He made a sudden movement toward the door of our mobile laboratory, obviously to help his friend and put an end to the carnage, but I stopped him before he could exit. I grabbed him by the collar, shook my head, and held my stun gun inches away from his throat.

"It is not our place to intervene."

#2 knew I meant business. He slowly took his seat next to a stupefied #1. I went back to researching The Subject.

I was a little surprised it had taken #2 so long to say enough was enough. But still, I couldn't have him acting on his emotions. I couldn't have him interfering with my experiment.

The only person that should've been acting on his emotions was The Subject. And he was doing quite well with that.

He continued to do so when he grabbed The Library Manager's keys from the floor, put them between his fingers while making a fist with the pointed sides facing out, and proceeded to hammer away and rip apart The Library Manager's throat. The sound and sight of flesh tearing and blood erupting was enough to make #2 vomit inside our mobile laboratory. This I considered to be incredibly unprofessional. He nearly heaved on my shoes. I knew I would have to reprimand him later for this.

While I stared down #2, out of my peripheral, I saw The Subject sever The Library Manager's carotid artery and destroy his esophagus. The Subject was so aggressive he almost decapitated his former boss. It was safe to say that The Library Manager no longer felt pain in his arms or leg. He would no longer feel pain ever again. With his head nearly sawed off and his neck torn wide open, The Library Manager became nothing more than The Subject's second victim.

NOTE #6
KAREN: *Why don't you think #2 put up more of a fight?*
DR. RAVENSDALE: *My stun gun.*
KAREN: *Yes, but maybe he could've wrestled it away from you.*
DR. RAVENSDALE: *#2? Wrestle the stun gun away from me? You can't be serious. He didn't have the balls to do something like that. He was too fretful. He was anxious about everything. I recall overhearing him cry to #1 about being an accessory to murder, although that was never the case. He said it made him feel trapped.*

KAREN: And that doesn't make you feel remorse? You don't feel bad for trapping your colleague?

DR. RAVENSDALE: You should ask #1 that very same question.

Blood was everywhere and continued to seep from The Subject's lifeless victims. Large areas of the carpeted floor were covered with gore. Various books and tables were splattered. The Subject was particularly stained. It would be a lot scrubbing for me and my team. But it was worth it.

I had learned so much from this test.

I had learned just how dependent on technology The Subject had become. I had learned that perhaps nothing would get in the way of that addiction.

A couple of lives were lost during this discovery, but, well, I'm sure you've heard the old favorite about the omelet and broken eggs.

But it's true.

It was a must for me to get somewhere genuine and meaningful with my experiment. And if some had to perish for the sake of that research, then so be it.

Their families should be proud. To have a loved one pass in the name of such radical revelations is tremendously honorable.

My experiment made them memorable. I've essentially provided those who've died with legendary status.

I know people will someday thank me for this. Perhaps even the families of the "victims."

***

An amazing thing took place once The Subject realized there was no further need for violence. Once he understood that The

Library Manager and The Older Woman were gone, The Subject's breathing went from heavy and frenzied to calm and steady.

Blood-splattered yet totally composed, still crouching over what used to be The Library Manager, The Subject dropped the set of keys and moved his finger toward the open neck. It was a very slow process. One that #2 couldn't watch, as he covered his face with his trembling hands.

With a look that wasn't one of distress or sorrow, but one of interest, The Subject wanted to inspect The Library Manager's open wound. But he held back his examination, stopping himself just a few inches away from the neck.

It wasn't fear that stopped him. Nor was it revulsion. It was the realization that whatever he wanted to find could actually be discovered through much easier methods.

The Subject lifted himself off the maimed body and steadily strolled to the computer area. He stepped over The Older Woman's corpse and took a seat in front of the monitor. He brought up the search engine and typed the words: *Death. Neck. Cut.*

He clicked the first page that came up and began reading intently. Like a young scholar oblivious to the death around him, the death that he created, The Subject read and continued to search the internet without any other care in the world. He could not have been happier.

My team and I remained in the mobile laboratory for a bit, dwelling on our next course of action. Swiftness was certainly a top priority, especially since we didn't want someone walking in and seeing what took place. But we still needed to be thoughtful and do all we could to avoid miscalculation. We didn't want to rush and forget a piece of easily traceable evidence.

As if any of that matters now.

I knew we would be able to bury the bodies once we got them back to the laboratory. That would be our easiest duty. That left us mulling over our most difficult task: making sure the library was as clean as possible.

I'm not stupid. I understand plenty about forensic evidence. I'm aware that no matter how much we cleaned, trace amounts of DNA would still be sprinkled throughout the library. But what else could I do?

The alternative, which was far from ideal, was to light a match and burn down the library. It wouldn't have been difficult, given the amount of flammable material, but I felt that route would've hurt in the long run.

Investigators can learn they are dealing with arson just as fast as they can learn they were dealing with murder. So I felt we had no other choice but to lean on option #1. It would provide the least conspicuousness.

After we cleaned from top to bottom, I figured we would lock up and leave a note on the front door saying the library was temporarily shut down. By doing so, people would initially believe The Library Manager to be ill and resting at home.

As time went on, people would surely start asking questions and think that he disappeared, which is when an official investigation would begin.

But I felt by that time we would be far removed from the situation and pretty much in the clear.

I expressed this to my colleagues and they agreed, although nervously.

#2 and I made our move to the library. #1 went to the nearby shopping market to purchase cleaning materials. I felt more comfortable sending #1. He was proving to be a much more loyal assistant. Plus, I felt it was important to keep #2 within sight.

#2 and I entered the library, locked the door behind us, and made our way to The Subject, passing the outrageously demolished bodies on the floor. I'll never forget #2's expression. His face, which was covered in tears from seeing his dead friend, also exhibited utter repulsion. It was as if he had never worked in a hospital. It was then that I started to grow sick of him.

I was gripping my stun gun behind my back as we arrived next to The Subject. My tone was calm yet stern as I said, "It's time to go."

I shifted my weight and prepared myself for battle.

This was unnecessary since The Subject slowly nodded his head and turned off the monitor. He then stood up from the chair and placed his hands by his sides like an obedient solider. It was then that I started to grow proud of The Subject.

He was turning into quite the lab-rat.

I told The Subject to wait by the front desk. His former workplace. #2 and I set out collecting our concealed video and audio equipment. Well, I did most of the gathering since #2 couldn't stop his tears and was finding it difficult to focus.

I ignored this and packed up the gear, checking off my list one by one, making sure not to overlook a single item.

A knock was heard from the front door just as I finished packing the equipment. Although it was the sound of a prearranged knock, #2 still looked concerned. The Subject didn't move a muscle. I moved toward the door and saw that it was in fact #1 with the cleaning supplies. I unlocked, brought him in, relocked, and went back to work.

We scrubbed to the best of our abilities.

The body fluid was still fresh, which made it easier to absorb. There was plenty that soaked into the carpeting, but that was unavoidable. Luckily, the carpeting was dark brown, so after our meticulous cleaning, if one wasn't deliberately searching for a crime scene, the place looked practically innocent.

We wiped the desks and countertops. We wiped the chairs and books. We wiped each and every item in that library just to make sure that most of the bloodstains and fingerprints were removed. Then I sent #1 to pull our mobile laboratory up front.

#2 and I first grabbed The Older Woman's body, which we wrapped using one of the tarps purchased by #1, and brought it to the mobile laboratory. Once that body was secure, we returned to repeat the process with The Library Manager. This trip wasn't as easy since #2 began weeping over his dead friend.

It was wretched.

Not wanting to deal with his weakness, I viciously grabbed #2 by the sides of his head and squeezed while staring into his eyes, waiting for him to knock it off.

This did the trick.

While carrying The Library Manager's corpse toward the exit, I stopped at the front desk and asked The Subject, "Are you ready?" He nodded and followed us outside.

We loaded The Library Manager's body without a single witness popping up. I turned back briefly to lock the front door with the sticky keys as #1 restarted the engine. I locked up, turned back to jump into the passenger seat, closed the door without a slam, and reclined as the mobile laboratory drove off.

The ride back was silent.

#1 seemed focused on his driving.

#2 was crying ever so softly.

I was elatedly thinking about the day's results.

The Subject was back on his tablet, searching the internet. The smile on his face was slight, but it was there.

Test #2 – The Date

With Test #2, I'll say that I did not want to turn out that girl's light. It was never my plan to get so involved. But there was no other way, you see. I couldn't have one solitary problem ruining the rest of my experiment. Actions had to be made…

More on this in a bit.

The first major test was in the books.

I was extremely pleased with the results. Whether he knew it or not, The Subject was revealing what it meant to live a life entirely connected with technology. Fantastic. Just Fantastic.

There was still much more to learn. But I felt everything was moving in the right direction. Minus a couple of speedbumps.

I'm of course talking about the two dead bodies from the library.

But that situation was actually easy to manage. Once we arrived back at the laboratory, after unloading the gear and bringing The Subject down to the basement, who in turn sprinted to his laptop, #1 and I brought the bodies to the backyard and buried them in one hole.

One hole.

It was relatively simple considering that I found no need to dig two holes.

But that doesn't make me a bad person.

I am not a monster! Do not listen to what these damn papers have written about me!

I am not callous.

I am someone who will do whatever necessary to accomplish my job in the most resourceful manner.

Now that you can feel my work ethic, you should understand how easy it was for me to successfully move on to my next test, which, as I'm sure you can imagine, took a great amount of planning.

The first step was to slightly rearrange The Subject's mentality. With Test #1 I made him watch a lot of work-related videos. However, to some extent, I also allowed him to watch other material, like all of those karate and street fighting videos.

I was the one making the schedules, but he still had options. There would be none of that for Test #2.

This would be a much more precise test.

The Subject would need a very fixed routine. One that involved pumping him with nothing but pornography.

I had previously shown The Subject pornography, but this was during a period of trial and error. It took place as he was just on the brink of his teenage years. I showed him various erotic encounters to learn more about his sexual orientation. I learned that he was heterosexual.

Some have called this part of my process extreme. Not me. I've very glad I did this, especially when the time arrived to utilize the information.

***

The first step with launching Test #2 involved decorations. I needed The Subject's environment to capture and influence his senses. I needed him to be fully focused on the task at hand. I needed him to think of nothing but sex.

Full coverage was essential.

I decorated each wall of the basement, every single inch, along with the ceiling and the floor, in erotic prints and posters. Some were a bit subtle. Others were blatantly explicit.

There was plenty of penis imagery in that basement. Large erect penises stuffed inside the orifices of dead-eyed woman.

I did utilize more indirect material as well. Not necessarily pornographic pictures, but posters that were nonetheless sexual. Like advertisements many would see during a movie trailer or on a large billboard.

One of the pictures I used involved a woman wrapping her red lips around a gleaming cherry while in her free hand she held a frozen phallic-looking treat.

There was another poster in the basement of three women on a beach; all dressed in white two-piece swimsuits and translucent cotton tank tops, playfully throwing water at each other.

I recognized the point of the advertisement. I was hoping The Subject would understand it as well. I was hoping The Subject would see that poster and get cravings for the women's bodies to become wetter, then think of their vaginas becoming wet, then think about entering each and every one of those wet vaginas.

I wanted him to have that passion.

This is why I covered the entire basement with such pictures. The Subject's possession of sexual desire was key if I was to learn about relationships in the age of technology.

Was I cheating?

Was I being unprincipled by using these posters since the images were on paper and not on a screen? I don't believe so.

The posters were nothing more than tools to keep The Subject motivated. Secondly, it's not like I didn't use the computer as well. I assure you I did. But patience, my dear. We will get to that shortly.

Along with the posters enhancing the basement, I also purchased a state of the art silicone love doll. This silicone love doll was rather costly, clocking in at nearly four thousand American dollars. But, for what was essentially a toy, the look of it came remarkably close to a human being. Most importantly, it was there for whenever The Subject felt prepared and aroused.

How did I acquire all of these items and not draw attention? How did I do this without seeming depraved?

The internet.

I found numerous sites that had everything necessary for this test. Then, after some resistance and begging from #2 not to do so, I used his credit card to purchase everything. #2 kept complaining about online records and how they never disappear. He said he didn't want his personal information connected to such "filth."

I fired back: "Filth? So I suppose our cutting-edge experiment has become nothing more than filth?"

This silenced him long enough for me to place the order.

I was beginning to consider #2's attitude disgusting and counterproductive. So yes, in a way, I suppose it was vindictiveness that moved me to use his credit card. Perhaps it was even some form of punishment. Penance for acting the way he did during the first test.

One way or another, #2 would learn that this experiment was bigger than him.

NOTE #7

KAREN: *Do you think #2 knew you were being calculatingly spiteful?*

DR. RAVENSDALE: *Yes.*

KAREN: And why do you say that?

DR. RAVENSDALE: Because of his glances. I could tell by the way he sometimes looked at #1. It was as if he was asking, "Why is he treating me this way?"

KAREN: Do you think you were being unfair? I mean, this was the same person you handpicked for your experiment.

DR. RAVENSDALE: It is very easy to lose respect for someone who once had potential.

The next phase of this test involved The Subject's injections. And I don't mean medication.

There were those shots as well. There had to be. It was a must to get The Subject back on a nocturnal routine.

But the injections I'm writing about now were in relation to the brain.

I monitored and led The Subject in the right direction for our first test. But on this go I really grabbed the bull by the bollocks and took total control.

With twenty-four hour surveillance, me and #1 taking shifts, we were able to make sure that The Subject wouldn't watch or read anything unrelated to pornography. I wanted nothing but sex injected into his psyche.

This was tricky at first.

The Subject regularly tried to go off track and search other areas. This is when my stun gun would come into play. All I had to do is show him the device. This would turn him back into a well-trained creature.

Not to mention, as I anticipated, once The Subject's sexuality finally formed and strengthened, he became completely immersed and wanted to search for nothing but erotic material.

But it took him a while to get to that point.

The process started off slow.

I brought a television down to the basement, which was locked within a glass case so The Subject couldn't turn it off, and I continuously played softcore pornography. Over and over and over and over, good-looking bodies grinded up against each other in an attempt to excite the viewer.

I played these videos for The Subject.

I had no time for sexual arousal. All I wanted to do was keep my eyes on The Subject.

I wouldn't say he was frightened. But he was certainly cautious at first.

During the beginning of this test, The Subject deliberately distanced himself from the television. He would stand approximately fifteen feet away and stare at the action. Not scared. Yet far from confident. Unsure. Yet fairly mesmerized.

Whenever the action on screen increased, The Subject would shift his weight back and forth while incessantly bobbing his head. He would occasionally make a movement as if he was ready to approach the television, but something would stop him, and he would return to his original position.

Whenever there was a lull in the film and sex was not taking place, The Subject became uninterested and steadily paced around the basement, glancing at all the posters, remaining at least fifteen feet away from the television.

These were the moments he seemed the most spellbound. Perhaps it was the pornography music playing in the background. All of the films used the same music and all the songs sounded as if they belonged on the weather channel. It had a mesmerizing effect.

The Subject would also occasionally approach the love doll, though throughout the first few weeks of this test he wouldn't do much. He typically stared at the doll, sometimes standing upright, sometimes crouching real close to the object, kind of like a jaded police detective who had seen too much on the job.

There were other days where he'd have a different approach.

With the back of his fingers, ever so softly, he would sometimes gently stroke the love doll's entire body. All the way from its toes to its scalp. Some might call the maneuver sensual. But watching The Subject perform this act made me think of the word: vulturine. It was as if he was telling the doll, "Soon enough. Soon enough."

The Subject's inspection of the doll increased as the weeks of Test #2 continued. The more he studied the more I felt it was time to raise the bar. Slowly but surely, I replaced the softcore pornography with films that were more hardcore.

Very hardcore.

I never knew stuff like this existed prior to the experiment. I initially found the material discombobulating. It was difficult to tell if the women in those videos were enjoying the action or if they were being injured. The erotic exploits seemed tremendously violent.

There was always loads of shouting, smacking, and biting. The heavy breathing alone made it seem as if the women were suffocating. I found out quickly that there is a big jump from softcore to hardcore pornography. It was an entirely different ball game.

The Subject instantly noticed this.

The level of comfort he developed had decreased the moment I switched the style of film. We had hit a period where he was beginning to inch closer to the softcore pornography. Where he was starting to appreciate it. But he rapidly recoiled once the hardcore material came into play.

He stood further back from the television than when the test first began. He also had problems looking at the screen for longer than two seconds. It was too much for him to handle. An overload.

I figured he just needed an adjustment period. Time to acclimate to the aggressive footage. But the hours turned into days and the days turned into weeks and he didn't become more comfortable. The more the hardcore material played, the more The Subject attempted to escape.

He of course could never fully get away since the television was locked in a glass case, making it impossible for The Subject to ever turn it off. But sometimes he would squat down in one of the corners of the basement while holding his fingers in his ears, closing his eyes tightly, and rocking back and forth while emitting loud hums, trying his best to drown out the noise.

This was unacceptable.

It would not stand. It *could not* stand. I had an experiment to run and I needed certain events to occur for the test to make an impact.

Yes, I know. The Subject's fainthearted reaction to the hardcore pornography exhibited his natural mindset. And this reaction showed that my test was working to a certain extent…

…No!

This wasn't good enough!

#2 was the one who said The Subject's reaction was a positive one. He went on to say that we were viewing the absolute truth. After #2 said this I informed him that he possessed the opinions of a daft peon. He shook his head and stomped off to another room, where I assume he sulked like a ridiculous man-child.

But I was right!

My experiment required something larger, much bigger than The Subject sitting in the corner of the basement trying to block the noise. To create a momentous experiment one requires momentous results.

Whether #2 agreed with me or not was none of my concern. I know it was right for me to do what I eventually did. I really believe this! And I really believe people will not only accept my decisions in the years to come but admire them as well!

How could they not?

Knowing the need for a bigger reaction, I thought of ways to push The Subject in the right direction. My first thought was to make him stand still in front of the television by threatening him with my stun gun. But I didn't want to keep going down that route. I didn't want to overuse that weapon and have its intimidation evaporate.

That was out of the question.

Thinking back to Test #1 made me realized that I also didn't want to stand over The Subject and struggle with holding his eyes open.

Then I thought of another plan. A far better one.

The idea hit me suddenly and with intense force. I knew it was a good strategy because, as soon as I thought of it, I felt a surge of excitement that lifted all of my hair and left my body tingling. I imagine it's a sensation akin to what sexual folks feel when watching pornography.

The solution brought me back to my years in England.

It was 1971.

Without friends, my options for amusement were limited. I didn't go to extravagant restaurants. I was too young for the pubs, not that I ever went when I reached proper age. That was reserved for socializers and addicts. Plus, I never acquired a taste for the pint.

There were never any clubs or rallies that interested me. So my move for pleasure always involved the cinema. This, of course, were the days before I started donating sperm.

The cinema I patronized was a cramped and shadowy little structure. Only a few lights ever worked and the staff was staler than the refreshments they served. There were never many others in the screening rooms, but somehow, there was always some amorous couple in the back row kissing and caressing each other as if they were in the privacy of their own home.

I found this infuriating.

Behavior of that nature is always intrusive and discourteous.

Simply because this couple found in each other someone they thought they loved, didn't mean they had the right to shove their delightful lives in the faces of others.

Oh, how it drove me up the wall!

I wanted to do terrible things to the couple behind me on that fateful day in 1971. But the more the film played, the less I cared about the pair. It was amazing. I became totally spellbound by what was taking place on screen.

The film playing that day was *A Clockwork Orange*. A film I had to sneak into due to my age.

Prior to seeing the film, I had heard and read how the adaptation was created as a sort of social protest against medical experimentation. Ha! I did not see it that way. I believed that analysis to be a lame circumvention. I still believe this.

What did I see?

I saw the gloriousness that played on screen to be a bold assessment regarding the astonishing achievements that originate from pushing the culture to its limits and finding desirable and genuine answers concerning the world we occupy.

That is what I saw. That is what I felt.

When the film arrived at the scene where the doctors locked the central character in front of a film screen and clamped his eyelids open, leaving him no choice but to view the footage, I was blown away by the overall brilliance.

The doctors were well aware of the struggle they'd receive from their patient, but they refused to be stopped by any difficulty. They made sure their experiment would move forward as planned!

I was inspired by the doctors in that film. Very much so. I was particularly motivated by their eyelid clamp design. It's no surprise that I eventually used that very same design to help me with The Subject.

Following much deliberation between myself and my colleagues, deliberation where #2 attempted to argue with me, #1 shrugged his shoulders a lot, and I told both of them they'd be foolish not to follow my lead, I entered the basement and injected The Subject with a large dose of Butorphanol. I didn't want him functioning while I installed the clamps.

Once I injected The Subject, which I did as he was sitting on his computer chair with wheels, I pushed him over to the glass case and stationed him two feet in front of the television screen. Then I locked those very same wheels.

Next object used was the long rope found in the shed. We used this to tie The Subject securely to his seat. #1 tied the knots. Nice and tight. The Subject would not be going anywhere. Not unless I wanted him to.

I then attached a makeshift brace to the back of The Subject's chair, one that would securely hold his head in place. This way he wouldn't be able to turn away from the screen.

Then came the eye clamps.

I have this peculiar thing about eyes. I wouldn't call it a phobia. But getting close to them, or having someone close to mine, gives me weak knees. Since I trusted him at that point more than the other colleague, I had #1 install the clamps and make sure The Subject would not be able to close his eyelids.

With that, our apparatus was complete.

With his eyes propped open and the Butorphanol beginning to subside, The Subject steadily returned to a conscious state. But I needed him even more alert, so I injected him a dose of Pentedrone. Blasted him with energy.

The result was stupendous.

The Subject went from lethargic to maliciously awake in the matter of seconds. Confused and full of power, yet realizing his inability to move more than an inch, The Subject became enraged.

He violently shifted in his seat as much as possible, which wasn't much. Unable to properly express his rage, he began snarling and shouting arbitrary sounds while foaming at the mouth.

Feeling panicked, #1 and #2 took three steps back from The Subject. I moved closer. I was intrigued and wanted to study him as much as possible. I had given him Pentedrone injections before, although never in such a large amount, but I have never witnessed such a reaction.

I arched lower, supporting myself with my hands on my knees, and put my face inches away from The Subject. I saw the sweat forming on his brow. His nostrils flared resentfully. His breath reeked something awful. In front of me was nothing more than a caged animal.

Unexpectedly, The Subject concluded his outburst and became silent. Very silent. He looked directly into my eyes for what must've been thirty or forty seconds, and then, like a damaged pipe bursting beneath a corroded sink, The Subject exploded with sobs.

It's peculiar to see someone cry without the ability to close their eyes or conceal their face. When one cannot guard themselves, they become almost whimsically illuminating.

That was The Subject. A man who could feel yet could not hide.

After a while of me staring at him, all without ever saying a single word, The Subject's sobbing finally stopped. I wouldn't say he calmed down. It was more like he ran out of steam.

This is when it finally happened.

For the first time throughout the experiment, The Subject spoke to me. Not to #1. Definitely not to #2. No way in hell that was happening.

He looked into my eyes as he mumbled his statement. The words were weak and insecure.

The Subject whispered the words, "Please. Just…Please."

I could feel my colleagues stepping forward. But I didn't care about their excitement or concern or whatever it was they were feeling at that moment. I only cared about the connection between myself and The Subject.

His words made me smile.

That smile must've done something for The Subject. His breathing began to balance out. I didn't like that.

Once I noticed his composure I immediately returned to an upright position and grabbed my colleagues by their arms to lead them out of the basement, leaving The Subject tied to the chair.

The Subject's anxiety reappeared, as well as his aggrieved whimpering. I slammed shut the basement door.

The crying went on for a long time. Two hours, seven minutes, and twenty-four seconds to be exact. I had figured, much like a baby, that he would have made himself exhausted way before he reached the first hour. I was wrong. His endurance was impressive.

My plan really developed once the crying finally waned.

What I did was leave him sitting in silence. Almost no stimulation for The Subject. The television was off. The computer was out of reach. The only thing he had were the posters lining the basement. But once I turned off the lights The Subject was left with nothing but his own boredom.

That was a major part of my strategy.

With all of that dullness, The Subject understood that he had virtually no control over what took place in the basement. This was a deliberate move on my end. I wanted him so bored and fidgety and apprehensive that no matter what I showed him next he'd feel not only indebted but also ardent. I needed him passionate.

I made sure this period of silence lasted for exactly three days, six hours, forty-two minutes and seventeen seconds. I would periodically feed, hydrate, and inject him, but I would do it all without ever saying a word.

I would inject him to go to sleep, then inject him to wake up, never providing him with more than four hours of sleep per night. No need for any more than that.

As for bathroom habits, I gave The Subject a blocker to stop his bowel movements. When he was sleeping I put in a catheter for him to urinate. I couldn't have him being untied and unclamped whenever he needed to relieve himself. That would've been disruptive.

NOTE #8

KAREN: The Subject never complained or tried to convince you to stop your actions? It's easy to believe that he might try. You were literally altering the way his body should function.

DR. RAVENSDALE: This seems to be one of the things that draws so much negativity from the papers. But what no one ever points out is how well The Subject was able to adjust. His adaptability was something Darwin would be proud to witness.

KAREN: Still, you never once had the impulse to see him free?

DR. RAVENSDALE: Set him free? You say this as if he was a prisoner. I'm the prisoner. He was a lab rat. If I placed him outside and said, "Go on," he wouldn't have known what to do with himself. I was the one who provided him with knowledge. I was his reason for everything.

The time arrived to bring Test #2 into full swing. The Subject was sleeping when I made this decision. I brought him around with another large dose of Pentedrone. His tolerance was beginning to grow. I was having to up the dosage fairly often.

Life and energy entered his body with a bang. It reminded me of a restrained horse finally released at the starting line. He began rocking and grinding so much that I thought he might snap his ropes. That didn't happen.

He might've had the liveliness, but he didn't have the strength of a horse.

Once The Subject adjusted to the injection, I leaned in and whispered, "No more mucking about. Are you ready to get serious?"

The Subject didn't respond.

Although his eyes were clamped open they somehow seemed to widen. No further hint of anger, which I was pleased to see. Perhaps there was even a bit of curiosity.

Above all else, he didn't shake his head after I asked about his readiness. He exhibited no sign of unpreparedness for whatever I had to offer. He seemed willing to follow my lead.

That's at least how I saw it.

I told him, "good boy."

I then turned to the television, started the DVD, and turned back to The Subject with fire in my core. Within the matter of seconds out blasted the hardcore sounds of very explicit pornography. I stood in front of the screen at first, deliberately blocking The Subject's vision.

I wanted him to see my face, to see my features, to know how significant I considered this test. I wanted him to *feel* how little tolerance I had for anything but the best results.

While the sexual screaming and gagging and slapping and moaning and howling and grunting and spitting and slurping and pumping blared behind me, I leaned in once more, placed my hand on The Subject's shoulder, which made his body release a slight shudder, and said, "Do not disappoint me, son. You do *not* want to disappoint me."

I turned away and exited the basement. The roaring sounds of pornography reverberating off the surrounding walls.

When I got back upstairs to the video monitors, #1 and #2 were somewhat watching the feed but also tensely looking in my direction. They were discernibly uncomfortable.

I attempted to ignore the bizarre atmosphere as I took my seat to focus on the monitor. But the feeling in the air was too abnormal. Almost awkward. I tried once more not to concentrate on it. I would've succeeded if #2 didn't speak up.

"Don't you..." #2 began, before pausing the type of pause that left me incensed. "Don't you think you are..."

"I *think* all the time." I interrupted. "And I *think* it would be wise for you to do a little less talking and a little more thinking yourself."

He went silent after that remark.

Wonderful silence.

I knew he was going to ask: *Don't you think you are getting too close?*

Firstly, I didn't need to answer #2's questions, especially if they were questions that involved such idiocy. Secondly, I didn't think I was getting too close to The Subject. Not at all. In fact, I thought it was time for me to move even closer to the experiment.

Second after second, minute after minute, day after day, I blasted hardcore pornography in The Subject's face. It was initially too much for him to handle. He squirmed a lot. Tried his best to escape. But all the struggling was useless. He had no other choice but to accept the erotic imagery.

The Subject's screams began after the first few days of watching videos. It was all nonsense. He never formed comprehensible phrases. Just a lot of raspy sounds.

I let him shout for a while, figuring at some point he'd get it out of his system. But that process took a little longer than expected.

He would fall silent whenever I went to feed him or give an injection. But his screams would start back up once I left the basement.

A week and a half of that madness was all I could take. I needed to come up with a plan that would remedy the situation.

I grabbed two socks and a roll of duct tape.

I might have been improvising, but it worked to perfection.

Back in the basement, I stuffed one of the socks inside the other, rolled the two socks into a ball, shoved the ball-sock into The Subject's mouth, and wrapped several rounds of duct tape around his head, making sure the gag held steady.

The Subject once again tried to squirm. He screamed muffled shrieks.

This only made me laugh.

I also remember wishing that The Subject could see the bigger picture. But that simply wasn't happening.

The Subject couldn't understand what was taking place. He couldn't understand his own importance. The Subject couldn't understand how imperative his participation was for my experiment. And he couldn't fully understand just yet that I would let nothing get in the way of my discoveries.

But he would learn.

Yes, he would learn.

Fortunately, it only took The Subject three days to comprehend the one way to get rid of the sock-gag. This was complete silence. Perhaps the gag had dried his mouth too badly. Perhaps it was hurting his jaw. Or maybe he had cooled off from not being able to hear his own screams and was finally able to make a rational decision. Whatever the case, I was pleased about his eventual cooperation.

Once I removed the gag it was pretty much smooth sailing.

The Subject initially watched the hardcore pornography since there was no other choice. But then came a moment. A wonderful moment. My colleagues claimed they didn't notice it. But the moment certainly occurred.

It started with a slight spasm of The Subject's left eye, as much as it could twitch given the clamp. And then, as if some mental light switch was flicked, both of his eyes went from being disoriented to enthusiastic. The pornography was working its charm.

I couldn't tell if his penis was aroused when the shift took place, but I could see that he had at least become interested. I felt myself breathe a sigh of relief. This test would go on the way I expected. The way I wanted.

***

After another week, The Subject was nearly foaming at the mouth. In a good way. He could not get enough of the sexual situations displayed on screen. He was so engrossed that he didn't even notice me when I entered to feed him or change his urine drainage bag.

We had arrived to a point where he would not turn away from the screen.

Once I knew he was hooked, day by day, I started loosening his ropes. I started around his ankles, then gradually made my way up his body until he was no longer tied to the chair. No longer a detainee.

If he wanted to, The Subject could've choked me right then and there. But he didn't. He couldn't concentrate on anything other than the pornography.

The last step was removing the eye clamps, which of course was handled by #1.

That was that.

The Subject was free to move.

Actually, I should say he was *sort of* free to move.

If he tried to escape the basement I would have brought my stun gun to his neck and tied him back to the chair. But that wasn't necessary. The Subject was becoming happy with his position in life.

The Subject finally left his chair two days after being untied. He tried to stand like a normal human, but being stationary for so long made his muscles temporarily dysfunctional.

The Subject's legs gave way and he fell to the ground, his body sending out a large thud upon impact. The fall looked like it should've hurt. But The Subject showed no signs of injury. He didn't even emit a single moan of discomfort. His mind was elsewhere. Too devoted to feel pain.

During the process of getting up from the chair, falling down, and being on the ground trying to work his muscles, The Subject's eyes never left the television. They were locked on the screen. Exhibiting pure hunger.

Once his muscles were capable of working, The Subject raised from the floor like a predator in the bush and stepped toward the screen. He placed his hands on the glass case while steadily moving his face closer and closer. Ever so slightly, his hips began to move. The effort was minor yet smooth.

Over time, as one video bled into the next, The Subject's movements became more aggressive. More striking. Since television's glass case was on wheels, The Subject gradually humped the box all the way across the room until it stood against a wall.

The Subject then humped even harder, rocking the glass case against the poster-covered wall. Worried that he might break the television, I readied myself to run down to the basement. But just as I stood up, The Subject suddenly stopped slamming the case.

He took a step back from the television, his hips still moving and humping the air, while he intensely watched the video. The film playing at that moment involved two guys dressed in firemen hats and boots smacking their erect penises against the face of a young blonde woman dressed as a schoolgirl. The young blonde woman was on her knees with her tongue hanging out of her mouth.

She occasionally giggled as the penises smacked her lips.

The Subject made his way to the love doll, rapidly glancing back to the screen every couple of steps, as if he feared missing the action.

When he arrived at the love doll, he grabbed the toy by the hair and dragged it back to the television. He then started disrobing himself with his eyes still on the screen. It was a gradual process. Partially because he was tuned into the pornography. But also because I'm the one who usually dresses and undresses him, and he's somewhat ill-suited for the task.

When The Subject was finally naked he began imitating what he saw on screen. He loved smacking his fully erect penis against the love doll's plastic face, occasionally slipping it inside the mouth and trusting away, just as the two men did in the video.

When the video changed, so did The Subject's style. Seeing an actor anally penetrate an actress, The Subject became inspired to do the same to his doll. Spank across the ass, The Subject copied the maneuver. Vaginal pummeling. Check.

The Subject was even more barbaric than the actors he emulated. Always emitting overexcited howls to the point where I had to lower the volume on my headphones.

The Subject not only began thrusting as hard as he could, he also started giving the love doll little whacks across the face.

This was only the beginning.

The first time The Subject ejaculated was attention-grabbing, to say the least. I could tell he was on the brink by the look on his face as well as his rhythm. His expression turned into one of confusion as his tempo decreased.

Seconds prior to ejaculation, The Subject stopped moving his hips and his expression altered from confusion to uneasiness. His face looked as if he was asking one of two questions: "What is happening to me?" Or "Why is this happening to me?"

At the final second before his ejaculation The Subject produced three hurried and freaked gasps. The gasps reminded me of my father on his deathbed.

Then the rush took place.

The orgasm was undoubtedly pleasurable for The Subject. But there also seemed to be a feeling of doubt coursing through his body. It was as if he felt insecure about feeling good.

The Subject gently removed himself from the love doll. He stood in a still position for a while, completely naked, rubbing his chest while looking into the lifeless eyes of his toy.

Only once did he look at his softening penis.

It was actually more of a glance.

He looked down, saw the glistening tip, and hurriedly looked away. That was the last time he looked at his penis.

It was a case of confliction.

The manipulating of his member made him feel delightful. Yet, after the release, he wanted nothing more to do with the flesh that brought him such joy.

Until the next time, of course.

***

The Subject walked in circles after his first ejaculation. He didn't bother dressing. He remained stark-naked while circling and circling and circling, all the while keeping his eyes away from the love doll and the pornography.

I would soon learn that this was all part of The Subject's process.

Following each ejaculation, he would immediately distance himself from his partner and walk in circles. Large circles. Small circles. Imperfect circles.

I wound up seeing plenty of this process.

The circling was The Subject's way of fleeing his guilt. I'm still unsure on why he felt remorse in the first place. I've spent a lot of time thinking about this. But I've landed nowhere close to a good answer.

Once he eventually recovered from the guilt, The Subject would return to his position in front of the television and start the process over again.

Improvements were made over time.

At three weeks and two days after his first ejaculation, The Subject's circling time started to reduce. He was circling the basement thirty-seven times at that point. I'd say this was a great improvement when compared to the one hundred and two times he circled during the earlier stages.

The Subject was beginning to find comfort in his actions.

The test was working.

My test was working.

The Subject stopped circling the basement all together by his thirty-second of ejaculation. He had ejaculated three hundred and forty nine times at that point and had finally become unperturbed by his actions.

Instead of circling, once he was done with his love doll, he would stroll back to his chair and serenely take a seat. Those were the moments where I'd go down to feed him and replenish his fluids. I wanted him as healthy as can be, so to speak.

The Subject never looked at me during feeding time. He would only ever look at the television or his love doll. If it was the love doll, he would only ever gaze at it with animosity.

That was an interesting development.

In the matter of weeks The Subject went from a man embarrassingly withdrawn when it came to sex, perhaps even disturbed by the act, to someone who couldn't hide his abhorrence for the object that helped create his pleasure.

The more The Subject watched pornography and penetrated the love doll the more ferocious he became. His open palm turned into a fist as his delicate smacks turned into vicious punches on the doll's face.

I thought that maybe it had something to do with the plastic quality of the love doll. With its expressionlessness. I figured The Subject was becoming upset since the dolls eyes were lifeless and its appearance did not match the women on screen.

Wanting to better appreciate my experiment, I found pictures online of woman's faces and printed out three images. One happy face. One sad face. And another face in the midst of an orgasm. Then, on three different occasions, while The Subject was sleeping from an injection, I attached a printed out face to the love doll with scotch tape.

This did not improve The Subject's mood.

It only made him more explosive.

No matter the expression, happy, sad or orgasmic, The Subject did the same exact thing. While sadistically thrusting his penis into the love doll he would claw and punch and tear the paper face until it was nothing more than shredded pieces on the basement floor.

None of the faces survived The Subject's anger.

***

I had seen what I felt was essential.

It was possible my former colleagues felt different, though I'm not entirely certain. I had stopped asking for their opinions. Too many occasions had popped up during my experiment where they tried to swerve me off the proper course. Particularly #2.

I wasn't having it.

I couldn't be bothered with any fears or foolish theories that could jeopardize my experiment. Too much was riding on the results. I had to stick to my guns for the sake of humanity. This is why I did not listen when they tried to talk me out of the rest of Test #2.

Perhaps I should've just fired them right then and there. But I figured I could still use them for any heavy lifting.

There was also the matter of them already knowing too much. With that in mind, I wanted them close by.

The last thing I needed was for one of them to spitefully prattle on to some outside party and endanger my work.

But when it's all said and done, I suppose some of these concerns are what led me to do what I eventually did to #2.

This makes me wonder if it actually would've been easier to terminate their employment.

I don't know.

But I'll get to all of this later.

Back to the test.

Ignoring my colleagues disapproving moods, I began setting in motion the next phase.

I created a mental checklist of what I required. This list involved: A woman. Arguably the most important item. A location. One that would involve little to no people getting in the way. And lastly, a two-way communication device that would allow me to stay connected with The Subject.

It wasn't as if I would be coaching him throughout the process, but I knew there would be moments when The Subject would need my help.

I began with the easiest item. The two-way communicator.

All I had to do was find a proper seller online and purchase the device. I found one that sold for $198.79. That included shipping. Seemed fair enough. As if the price really mattered. They could've charged me four thousand dollars and that wouldn't have stopped me. No amount was too high for my experiment.

The second step involved finding the right location. Although slightly trickier and most costly, this too was a relatively easy task. The only aspect I didn't like was that we had to deal with an outsider.

We needed a *great* location for The Subject's date. I figured a restaurant would be an ideal spot. One that was small yet romantic, whatever the hell the latter meant.

As luck would have it, once he started breaking out of his disapproving mood, #1 informed me that he was the man with the connection this time around. He had a childhood mate who owned a restaurant only one hour and fifteen minutes away from the laboratory.

#1 was a bit hesitant though, considering what happened to #2's friend. But I convinced him that nothing of that nature would happen again.

On the flip side, when I explained my anxiety over the inclusion of an outsider, #1 assured me that he would keep details to a minimum with his connection.

I felt more relaxed after hearing that.

Now…what were these details?

Firstly, I required the ability to completely rent out the restaurant for the entire evening. Wanting to keep the number as low as possible, I also demanded that only *one* chef work the kitchen.

#1 went on to tell his friend that this was due to a much-admired yet very secretive individual wanting complete privacy while dining with his "girlfriend."

A lie, of course. But one that would work well.

Upon hearing this information, The Restaurant Owner informed #1 that the cost of rent for the evening was $8,500. He also said that if the price was met he would do all of the cooking himself.

This was fantastic.

Not only would the restaurant be empty, the owner would also be generally absent since he would be preparing the meals.

Done deal.

Acquiring the third item was the most difficult on the list. It wasn't like explaining the Dirac equation to someone with Attention Deficit Disorder, but there were a number of variables to consider. So I had to be extra alert.

I needed to buy a prostitute.

But it wasn't simple. I needed a whore who wasn't a drug addict, as many of them are, and didn't have a pimp.

A self-regulating whore, if you will.

Again, the last thing I needed was too many people privy to my test. Especially a pimp. Who knows what a criminal of that sort would do or say if he heard his worker was involved with a groundbreaking experiment. I bet someone like that would demand more money, which probably wouldn't keep his mouth shut for too long anyway.

Criminals disgust me.

And that was a problem I did not want to handle. I already had too much on my plate. The last thing I needed to fret about was a depraved pimp.

I expressed this concern and, stepping up once more, #1 mentioned how we could find a self-regulating prostitute on Craigslist.

I thought this was a great idea.

But it was also a plan that required my caution.

NOTE #9

KAREN: *Why do you think #1 was becoming so helpful at this point?*

DR. RAVENSDALE: *That's simple. He saw what was happening with #2 and he made a choice between being on the* *winning side of history or the losing side. He, at that moment, chose to go with me.*

KAREN: And that was the winning side, I assume?

DR. RAVENSDALE: I won't be answering such ridiculous questions.

Leaving The Subject locked in the basement with his pornography and his battered love doll, my whole team set out one day to find a usable computer. One that wouldn't be traced back to us.

We first stopped by the library that hosted Test #1. Well, it was more like we drove by.

Upon entering the parking lot, the first thing we noticed was the caution tape wrapped around the front of the library. As we rolled closer we spotted a sign posted by the police that read: Closed until further notice.

#1 drove out of the lot. #2 became jumpy and irksomely sweaty. I looked out the window from the back seat and shook my head.

I was more bothered with #2 than anything else.

I slightly understood why he was frightened, but that didn't mean I had to accept his juvenile conduct.

It was obvious that #1 was scared as well. But at least he handled it decently. He didn't tremble or let out a pathetic whimper.

Much like myself, he recognized that we had priorities and understood that there was no point to bitch and moan about past events.

#1 drove for miles until we reached the next library. We all entered upon arrival, but I was the one who took the lead.

I used my fake ID to sign in and gain access to the internet.

Most websites deemed filthy are blocked at places like the library. Fortunately, Craigslist is a permissible site since it's frequently used by people looking for work, even if said word is occasionally sketchy and commonly leads to only one quick pay day.

Adding to the luck, Craigslist is the type of site where individualism reigns supreme. The majority of people either looking for work or hiring are doing so in an independent fashion. Most big companies do not utilize the site, at least not habitually. For that reason, middlemen, like pimps, are removed from many scenarios.

I went on to Craigslist and searched the men seeking women page, as well as women seeking men, casual encounters, miscellaneous and romance.

The first thing I noticed while scanning was that many people were looking to sleep with someone of Asian descent. I also noticed that the search for enlarged labia was a constant theme on many message boards.

There were loads of posts about big labia.

I had to search for a while until I finally located and gathered five usable posts. Each of the five was similar in language. Always brief. Always worded just right. Always in a way where prosecution would be challenging.

All of them essentially said: If you're looking for a fun date, and want to be discreet, contact me with your information and we can go from there.

Out of the five posts, I narrowed the collection down to two. This was because three of them didn't have pictures. The two with pictures showed the posters' nearly naked bodies. One was black. The other white. Both women were skinny and had bulbous breasts.

I created a Gmail account with a fake name and messaged both craigslist contact e-mails. I kept my message simple, not wanting to generate any unwanted chariness, and told them that money was of no concern.

Then I waited.

I glanced around the library while continuously clicking the refresh button. #2 stood tensely by the exit. #1 perused the nonfiction section. The middle-aged librarian busied herself with her work. The only other three people in the library – all senior citizens – sat close to one another reading newspapers. They seemed very serene. Almost unaware of anything else taking place a few feet away from them.

A response came at last.

It was from the white woman.

She said that she was interested in a "date" and inquired about the next step. I responded that she should call me. I provided the number to my pre-paid cell phone. My burner, as journalists would later call it.

There was a moment when I thought about using both women. The white and the black. A triangular date. But I thought better of it, figuring it might be too much for The Subject to manage and could botch-up my test. So I didn't write back to the black woman when she later responded.

Looking back at it all now; I wonder if she knew just how close she came.

So close.

The white woman's second response said that she'd call in, "five minutes."

I sent back, "Perfect."

I signed out and gathered my colleagues.

We were back in our mobile laboratory driving home when my phone rang. The call came in nine minutes later than when she said she'd call. This tardiness enraged me. But I kept a cool head in order to make everything run smoothly.

The prostitute sounded mistrustful over the phone. Very cagey. She kept her sentences as brief as her craigslist post. She kept emphasizing that our arraignment was strictly a date.

"People think this is all about sex," she said, guarding herself in case I was a cop. "I don't know anything about that. That's not my business. I'm a professional *dater*. You understand that?"

I told her I understood.

But I didn't care what she called herself or what she did or didn't do with her clients. All I cared about was my experiment. To me, this whole test was about the social aptitude that develops or does not develop when a man has nothing but pornography as an educator.

That was it.

That was the end all be all.

This whore sleeping with The Subject was never the point.

And I can tell you without a trace of deceit that what eventually took place was not intended. I never imagined this test would go so far.

How could I imagine such things?

I'd have to be a psychopath.

I am not a psychopath!

Even so, I wouldn't declare that I'm remorseful. It is not my aim to be hard-hearted, but I still have to be genuine. And the truth is I would not have made my discovery if what eventually happened never occurred.

***

The prostitute and I hammered out the rest of the details, landing on a payment of fifteen hundred dollars for three hours of her time. This of course didn't necessarily mean that sex was included.

I told her the location of the restaurant and we settled on a date three days from our chat.

The next thing I did was go back to the lab and prep The Subject.

Much like the process for his job at the library, I bathed The Subject and gave him a haircut to go with a fresh shave. This was essential, for he was filthy and smelt like a decomposing rodent.

Another essential was the injections I provided to get him back on a normal routine of sleep and dining.

Schedules are good.

I needed The Subject on point, as sharp as possible for his big date with the whore known as: Pepper.

But the most important phase of The Subject's preparation involved the reduction of pornographic material. He was to be copiously desirous by the time he arrived at his date. However, much like the reduction method of an addict, I had to be careful not to pull the plug too swiftly.

A step by step approach was key.

I began by eliminating the posters from the walls, floor and ceiling of the basement. This removal was not met with hostility. The Subject was so focused on the television that he didn't even notice what was taking place.

The only time The Subject detected the activity is when #1 lifted him off the ground – without much effort, given that he only weighed 8.5 stones (roughly 120 pounds for those in the states) – so I could remove the posters beneath his feet. But The Subject didn't make a fuss about this either.

The next removal was trickier.

The process was complicated before it even started since my team and I had to decide what The Subject would miss the most: The television? Or the love doll?

Following much consideration, figuring that The Subject used the television as a motivator and thus needed that device more than anything else, I went with the removal of the battered and sticky love doll.

The Subject became alert when I grabbed the doll and moved toward the exit. I wouldn't say that he ran or lunged for his partner, but he surely moved faster than normal.

He reached out and grabbed the love doll's arm. Meagerly, almost tragically, he attempted to pull the doll away from my grip. With disconsolate eyes, The Subject looked at me and made whimpering noises, like a ruined dog begging for its toy. I returned his gaze with great passion and simply shook my head.

That was all I needed.

Nothing more.

The Subject knew not to disobey.

He dropped the love doll's arm and returned to the television with a raincloud of despondency above his head. I climbed the basement steps and locked the door behind me.

The withdrawal of the posters and the love doll took place in a single day.

The following day was devoted to removing the television, as well as handling any madness that might arise due to said removal. I was well aware that a simple shake of my head wouldn't do the trick this time. The Subject was too hooked on pornography to surrender without a fight.

I brought down to the basement my stun gun as well as my two colleagues. Just in case. But, out of all of us, I was the one who had a growing relationship with The Subject, so I felt it was right of me to offer my colleagues some advice. I told them to not use any sudden movements and to never raise their voices.

Naturally, #2 botched that.

Why wouldn't he?

We entered the basement little by little, all of us on the balls of our feet. The Subject was no more than twenty four inches away from the glass case, watching pornography while vigorously rubbing his crotch. He didn't notice our presence at first. It wasn't until #1 started to wheel away the glass case that The Subject snapped out of his zone.

But #1 handled the assignment well. He moved at a snail's pace and didn't make any jolting gestures.

While #1 gradually moved the case, I continually emitted low and soft shushing noises, as if to inform The Subject that all was okay and he had nothing to worry about.

It was working.

All was going according to plan.

That is until #2 grew impatient.

Breaking my rules, #2 let out an irritated exhalation, a groan that said, "Enough is enough," and sprang for the extension cord running through the small hole drilled into the glass case. Once he had the cord in hand, #2 yanked it out of the socket and cut out the pornography.

The Subject's response time was quite remarkable. There was *maybe* a second of eye contact between the two before rage hijacked the scene and The Subject savagely attacked #2.

Much in the way #2 lunged for the extension cord, The Subject charged at #2's arm, grabbed it firmly and sunk his teeth into the flesh, approximately ten inches up from the wrist.

#2 let out an ear-piercing shriek. This was another mistake on his behalf.

Upon hearing such a loud scream The Subject grew more flustered and moved up to #2's neck, clamping down while sadistically shaking his head.

The Subject bit and shredded like an unrestrained monster. #2 screamed for help like a damaged child terrified of death. #1 tried to pull his colleague away from The Subject. This only made matters worse. The Subject's clasp grew tighter and blood erupted over their three faces and rained down onto the basement floor.

#1 called out for me to help. I was deliberately slow to take action. I felt the punishment fit the crime. I warned #2. I warned him! I informed him of the right way to perform his tasks. Did he listen? No. Like a fool, he grew impatient and tried to accelerate the process.

#2 should've known better.

As my subordinate, he should've followed my guidance.

Seeing as this didn't happen, I had no problems letting his pain sink in a little while longer.

I waited until The Subject came up for air before I finally used my stun gun. I zapped The Subject several times before he dropped to a knee, then I hit him again, bringing him down to the floor at last. He convulsed spastically.

I zapped him once more for good measure.

Out of the clutches of The Subject, #2 dropped down to his knees and began desperately crying. Through his tears and his horrendous display of anguish I heard him squeak out, "I won't do this anymore! This has gone too far!"

I scoffed at his statements and told #1 to bring the wounded colleague upstairs. The time had come for stitches.

It's not that I cared about proper medical procedure, it's just that I could no longer set my eyes on his blood-splattered and swollen face. He looked pathetic.

A disgrace.

It was at that moment I started to formulate the strategy. The plan to get #2 away from my experiment.

After #2 was led upstairs, although it would interfere with the sleep schedule, I injected The Subject with a large dose of Butorphanol. I didn't need him creating any further issues.

With The Subject unconscious, I unlocked the glass case and grabbed the Television to bring the device upstairs. I then returned to the basement, dragged The Subject to his bed, uploaded a program on his devices to block all erotic content, and left him to sleep off the rest of the injection.

Preparing The Subject for his date was a lot of work.

#2 was given an injection once he was stitched and swathed in bandages. It was an injection I personally administered.

Shutting him up and stopping his incessant sniveling was advantageous since it meant that I only had to deal with noise coming from one end.

The low end.

The screaming coming from the basement were just as spine-chilling as #2's when his flesh was ripped open. The Subject was finally awake and completely lost without his pornography. He was disorganized. Frantic. Homicidal.

There wasn't much time left to prepare him for Pepper, but I knew I couldn't just rush down to the basement. I don't think The Subject would've done anything to me, considering I was pretty much in control of him, but I couldn't be 100% certain.

So for a couple of hours I let him do his worst all by his lonesome.

I needed him burnt out.

He paced and sprinted around the basement looking for the television. I didn't like this. It showed his level of intelligence to be subpar at best. Granted, he didn't see the television being removed, but there weren't many hiding places in the basement. This didn't stop him from searching like a coked-up bloodhound.

Finally realizing his search was hopeless, The Subject moved on to his computer and tablet to search for pornographic sites. He obviously came up with nothing.

Following six minutes of searching on both devices, The Subject lifted the computer monitor from the desk and made a motion to throw it across the basement.

He stopped himself right before releasing the monitor and gently placed it back on the desk.

This I liked.

It showed that somewhere deep down inside The Subject still had a modicum of mindfulness. It showed that he was aware of what the computer had done for him in the past. It showed he understood that the computer might be his only companion. This made him realize that he didn't want to destroy his one true friend, especially since that demolition would make him twice as lonely.

But this realization did not curb his fury. Once he placed the monitor on the desk The Subject made his way to his bed to remove the mattress to wreak havoc on the frame.

He broke it to bits.

He then took the shattered bits and destroyed those until he held nothing but dust. The bedstead was fashioned out of flimsy material, but I was still impressed with The Subject's determination.

The dismantling of the bedframe pacified The Subject.

I made my way down to the basement when The Subject sat down on the floor and his breathing went from hurried to stable.

#1 offered to join me, but I told him to stay upstairs to, "keep an eye on #2." This was me faking compassion. I didn't care about #2's condition. I just knew that #1's presence could have led to further issues with The Subject. I knew I would have better control of the situation if The Subject saw me by myself.

But that didn't mean I wasn't gripping my stun gun.

I entered the basement and locked eyes with The Subject. We stared for nearly a minute until, like a disciplined child, he broke the gaze and looked down at the basement floor.

What I did next was perhaps a bit ballsy. But I felt it was essential to push the limits and see how close to the edge I could go.

I approached The Subject and extended my hand. He could've bitten me like he did #2. He could have broken my arm or murdered me like he did The Library Manager and The Older Woman. But he did nothing of the sort.

He frailly placed his hand in mine and I raised him off the floor. I then put my fist on the top of his back, the one holding the stun gun, and guided him over to the computer.

I sat him down in front of the computer monitor and started playing videos detailing, "The Art of Dating."

The Subject seemed unenthused at first, probably since the men in the videos weren't pounding whorish women. But he wouldn't say a word to me about his displeasure. He knew better than that.

The Subject remained quiet as I left him to learn the ways of dating from men who seemed as if they did nothing but workout and bathe in cologne.

The men on the videos were well proportioned and, by society's standards, certainly good-looking.

And even though The Subject knew nothing about the fads of contemporary culture, I hoped that he would become aware of the men's coolness and become compelled to fully concentrate.

Crazier things have happened.

While upstairs I made my way over to #1. He was apprehensively examining his sleeping colleague.

#1 was completely rattled for the first time since the start of the experiment. I didn't like it.

Gradually turning his head from his colleague, #1 looked at me with uneasy eyes and said, "Do you think this has gone too far?"

#1 wasn't being aggressive. He wasn't asking in a pugnacious manner. He was asking me from a genuinely frightened place.

"What do you think?" I asked, wanting to appear considerate. "Do *you* think this has gone too far?"

"I don't know. I…I know what we're trying to do here and…"

"*Trying?*"

"No. Sorry. Not trying. I know what we *are* doing. And I know we're doing this for the greater good and all. I just…I just don't think I was ready for all this violence. Look at him," #1 pointed at #2. "Who's to say I'm not next? Who's to say I won't end up injured…or worse?"

The first thought that came to me was: There is nothing to say that won't happen.

I knew that violence could very well be in #1's future.

But I didn't say that.

I didn't say much. I knew if I tried to explain myself or the experiment to #1, or ask him for his opinion on what to do next, I would get nothing but undesirable results. So I kept it simple. I provided a line that would inspire him while also not allow him to retreat.

"Listen, you're doing a wonderful job," I told #1. "I would not be able to endure without your conscientiousness and intellect. And I'm glad I don't have to."

I paused to let that line penetrate.

"I know that some of the events in our experiment have been unfortunate. Even gruesome. But you must consider the results we've obtained. Think about all that we're achieving. Think of how our research will be remembered. How *we'll* be remembered."

I then placed my hand on #1's shoulder and gave it a tender squeeze. I held my hand on his shoulder for three seconds before turning away and moving back to the monitors to watch The Subject.

I couldn't coddle #1 for too long. There was real work to be done.

NOTE #10

KAREN: Do you think this display of compassion, even if a fake one, made #1 feel as if he had to stay?

DR. RAVENSDALE: Absolutely. People sometimes need reassurance, especially in the workplace.

KAREN: Yes, but this wasn't exactly a standard workplace. Maybe your colleague didn't need reassurance. Maybe he needed distance.

DR. RAVENSDALE: You're partially correct. The feeble always want to distance themselves from fluctuating situations. But that doesn't matter in this instance. There was nowhere for #1 to go. You have to remember that this experiment was a part of his life for nearly twenty years. It's difficult to remove oneself from something they've worked on for so long.

KAREN: Especially when they're an accessory to a number of crimes.

DR. RAVENSDALE: You see that. That right there. Accessory to a number of crimes. You judgmental twat. I didn't accept that from #2. And I won't accept it from you. What you see as crime I see as discovery.

KAREN: But can you understand why other people don't see it that way?

DR. RAVENSDALE: No. And I never will.

The day arrived!

It was time for The Subject's date.

I had been playing countless videos regarding guidance on socializing, as well as videos of actual dates from various reality TV programs, figuring these clips, mixed with the earlier sessions of pornography, would prepare The Subject both mentally and physically for his evening with Pepper.

I bathed and shaved The Subject once more as the time approached for us to depart. I wanted The Subject as fresh as possible. #2's dried blood on his face was not a good look.

As soon as the clock reached 6:45pm that evening, I attached the GPS tracker to The Subject and told #1 to load him into the mobile laboratory while I made sure #2 was settled for "another relaxing night in."

As the half-sedated Subject was being loaded into the vehicle, I took it upon myself to *fully* sedate #2.

Well, I went a bit beyond that.

I filled a syringe with a lethal amount of Arsenic, which I had the foresight to pack before moving to the laboratory, found a vein and injected #2 without a moment of hesitation. He was still sleeping when I injected him. He would never again open his eyes.

I believe I provided #2 with an undeservedly painless death. I provided a trouble-free death for a man that had become such a pain in the bullocks. A man who probably should've been tortured. This pissed me off. It still does!

But I made the right play.

The grisliness of a violent death would've lead to further issues, particularly with #1.

Following the fatal injection, I walked outside and entered the mobile laboratory. The van was put into drive and we went on our way.

***

Unbeknownst to The Restaurant Owner, cameras were arranged by #1 around the entire establishment. Total coverage. Just like the library.

I also had #1 reiterate to The Restaurant Owner that he would be serving a very high profile individual who wanted absolute privacy for his date, and that he should not speak with this individual, even whilst serving him.

Under no circumstances would he bother The Subject.

This was very important to me. I did not want another situation like The Library Murder. I felt a situation like that could occur if The Restaurant Owner said the wrong thing to The Subject. Or even made a wrong movement.

I was looking out for everyone's welfare.

Honestly.

As instructed, Pepper was standing outside the restaurant waiting for our arrival. She wore an incredibly low cut dress. One that also showcased a lot of leg. Quite whorish.

Not as instructed, her dress was more of a maroon color, although I repeatedly told her to wear one that was bright red. I found this error to be rather displeasing. Her inability to listen meant one of two things: either she couldn't pay attention to details, or she didn't care about specifics. Neither of those two possibilities were encouraging.

But I was willing to let it slide, especially since she at least showed up at the right location and the test could continue.

We parked in front of the restaurant and I prepared myself to conduct business. I told #1 to keep an eye on The Subject as I exited the mobile laboratory to speak with Pepper. As I approached, her gaze suddenly became suspicious and she looked as if she was about to hurry away. I interrupted any thoughts of escape by jumping into conversation.

"Pepper, correct?" I asked. "I'm here for the date."

"You're the one who called?"

"Yes."

"You sound different than you look?"

"There is no need to be nervous. Everything is okay."

"I'm not nervous," Pepper fired back, almost over sensitively so. "I just want to make sure you're not a cop. Not that I'm doing anything wrong. I'm just trying to see…"

"I'm not an officer, Pepper. I'm not even the person you're dating tonight."

"Wait. What's going on here? You're not the guy I spoke to?"

"I am. I'm just…"

"I think I should go. I don't think…"

Tension started to build.

"No, stay," I continued. "You don't need to go. There's nothing funny going on here. You spoke with me earlier because my son, the person you're dating tonight, is a tremendously anxious person."

Silence.

"This is why I set the whole thing up," I carried on. "I wanted him to meet a nice young woman who could crack him out of his shell."

"Really?" Pepper asked, slightly offended. "Isn't that…I don't know…*weird*? You know, since you're his father and all."

"No. It's not weird."

That's as far as my response went. I was in no mood to be judged by this woman. In no way would I explain myself to her.

No matter the lingo she used in relation to sex for money, this woman was a whore. Apparently just like my mother.

I had seen and dealt with plenty during my days at the hospital. Absolute cretins. Cesspits. Sordid excuses for human beings!

If I owed Pepper anything it was a swift chop to the back of her skull.

"Okay," She responded at last. "But I'm not doing any doubles."

"Doubles?"

"Yeah. I'm not *dating* both you and your kid. You know what I'm saying?"

"Sure. No doubles. I just want you to have a nice date with my son. Only my son. And if you happen to go any further with him I will gladly provide three times the initial price. Afterward of course."

"Three times more?"

"Yes."

"Okay. Well…let's see how everything goes. Where's the kid? Is he close by?"

"Yes. Go inside the restaurant and take a seat," I said pointing through the window at the only table arranged with red napkins and burning candles. "My son will join you shortly."

Pepper hesitated briefly before finally nodding and entering the restaurant. Through the window I saw her take a seat and begin glancing around apprehensively. I needed to act fast before she lost her nerve. Before I lost my test.

I rushed to the mobile laboratory and yanked The Subject to the sidewalk. He was acting like a lost child and his body moved like ragdoll. I didn't care. I didn't care that he was outside his comfort zone. We had an experiment to conduct and nothing would get in the way.

The final step before entering the restaurant was to place the two-way communicating device inside The Subject's ear. I choose the right ear since that would be the one facing the window and I'd be able to see if he tried removing it. I wasn't certain what I would do if that actually happened. But I was thinking it would involve severe punishment.

As I walked to the entrance my mind was moving rapidly, pondering if I should enter and escort The Subject to the table. I didn't want to be more involved than I already was, but I couldn't ignore The Subject's pulsating uneasiness. He had become extremely reliant on me. So I made the decision to lead him in, figuring it would help the test.

I remember hoping that The Restaurant Owner wouldn't appear from the back to try to make my acquaintance. The last thing I needed was for him to know any more than he needed. That fortunately did not take place.

My involvement was short and sweet. Well, maybe not sweet. It was perhaps a tad awkward.

Clutching The Subject's elbow and essentially lugging him to the dinner table, I told Pepper to remain seated and plunged into the introductions. I let each of them know about the other and specifically emphasized that they were on a date. I used the word *Date* four times during my introduction.

This was more for The Subject than Pepper.

I was trying to tap into The Subject's psyche. Into his memory. I wanted him to hear the word and recall the dating videos. I wanted him to remember how the people from the videos interacted with one another.

But as I stood at the table, leaning over The Subject, pushing his shoulder to keep him seated, I couldn't tell if any of the footage was registering. All seemed to be out of whack. The Subject kept his eyes on the white tablecloth while his right leg convulsed erratically. Not the best of signs.

But there was only so much I could do.

Not wanting to stay any longer and risk being seen, I closed out my involvement by looking directly into Pepper's eyes and whispered, "Make sure you both play nice."

Pepper needed to know that she would have to take control. The Subject wouldn't be of much use if she didn't push the date in the right direction. Her slow, almost petrified, blink seemed to say that she agreed.

With that I was off. Back to the mobile laboratory. Back to where the real entertainment would begin.

***

As if on cue, right as I took my seat in front on the monitor, The Restaurant Owner exited the kitchen to serve appetizers. It seemed too much like perfect timing. This upset me.

It seemed as if The Restaurant Owner was deliberately waiting until I left to serve his opening dishes. As if he had an eye on me the whole time.

Even if I was overthinking, it was a thought I did not enjoy. I didn't appreciate the idea of being watched without my knowledge of surveillance. It angered me then. And it angers me now.

I'm fairly certain there is a team of people watching me this very moment, possibly laughing as I struggle with this pencil in my mouth. That should not be happening. I should not be here. There should be no observation without my consent. And I most certainly should not be laughed at by a group of unacceptably amateurish, unqualified, ignorant assholes!

If these imbeciles had even a modicum of brainpower they would unshackle me at once and throw themselves down to kiss my feet. But I would not let them kiss. No! I would kick and kick and kick until every last one of their teeth dropped out of their blabbering mouths.

They would accept this fate because they would finally understand my virtuosity! My brilliance! They would understand that it is far better to be beaten by a genius than to be ignored by one.

And I would grant them this service without fail!

***

The courses were prearranged by me and communicated to The Restaurant Owner via #1. The appetizer was a suitably prepared plate of tomatoes and fresh mozzarella with a topping of basil leaves and vinegar.

The Subject made no move to the plate. This might have been due to his anxiety. Or it could've been because he had never seen such food and didn't know how or where to begin.

The Subject didn't know much at all about eating given that I had to basically force-feed him his meals.

Through our two-way communicator, I told The Subject, "lift the white food off the plate with your fork and bring it to your mouth." He did just that. But since I wasn't 100% specific he held the cheese in front of his closed lips like a terminated android.

Pepper considered this strange. She herself even froze a bit after seeing The Subject's behavior. The scene was uncomfortable.

I told The Subject to insert the cheese and tomato into his mouth, chew and swallow. But my instructions were of no use. He was now fully motionless. It was the eye contact with Pepper that did him in.

Dumbfounded by the eccentricity of her date, Pepper could not shift her eyes away from The Subject. Also unable to move, The Subject continued to lock eyes with Pepper. It was a far-from-passionate staring contest between two primates attempting to comprehend each other.

The gawking went on for a while.

It was occasionally interrupted when Pepper felt too awkward and glanced out the window, or looked down to bite the tip of her thumb. But whenever she looked up once more she was yet again seized by the stare of her date.

The Subject's gaze became progressively determined as time went on.

"Say something to her," I whispered in The Subject's ear. "Utilize the videos I showed you."

The Subject did not react to my advice. Not even a grunt. He continued to stare and sporadically shift his body left to right and right to left as if he was on a swaying ship.

Once The Restaurant Owner removed the barely touched appetizer and returned to his kitchen, unquestionably feeling the awkwardness between the patrons, Pepper finally attempted to break the ice.

"So," she began, her voice insecure. "What do you think of my dress?"

The sound of Pepper speaking disrupted The Subject's stare. Before she finished her question, he was looking down at the tablecloth and breathing heavily. Like a life-long smoker forced to sprint a mile of rocky terrain.

"Oh, it's okay," Pepper told The Subject, quickly softening her attitude. "There's no need to be nervous. Your dad told me you might be, but it's okay. I'm a nice girl. Come on. Look this way."

Her voice became soothing. It was a nice touch.

I knew the gentle approach would help The Subject. He always stopped to listen if the girl in a porno said something, especially if the statement was made in a sweet and tender tone.

This of course would be right before he applied all of his energy and madness on his love doll.

The entrees arrived but Pepper didn't seem to notice. She was doing her best to get The Subject's attention.

"Come on," she said. "What'd you think of my dress?"

As she asked this question a second time, she deliberately smoothed her hands over the front of her dress. Over her bulky, slightly saggy breasts. The breasts of a whore.

With that single motion Pepper became her true self. While making the deal with me over the phone, all the way up to when the entrees were served, Pepper could've gone on and on about how this was nothing more than a date. But she and I both knew the facts. We both knew that she was a woman that had sex for money. Indisputably so.

That wasn't the only thing revealed by her motion.

With that motion Pepper also revealed the great zeal of The Subject.

He caught the gliding movement of Pepper's hands and his eyes were now fully raised from the white tablecloth, locked in a new staring contest. One that involved Pepper's cleavage.

Pepper noticed his probing eyes and leaned closer to exhibit more flesh.

"Do you like what you see?"

The Subject didn't respond with words. He just snorted like a cave dweller. A dribble of spit fell from his mouth and onto the table.

Pepper didn't recoil. Being a whore had apparently taught her to accept all forms of unusual conduct.

The other person who saw this odd behavior was The Restaurant Manager. He was heading to refill the water just as The Subject began drooling. Being unsure of how his reaction would influence my test, I had a moment of jumpiness.

The Restaurant Manager was troubled, perhaps even appalled, but he didn't say a word. I had to give it to him. He remained loyal to his promise by keeping his mouth shut and heading back to the kitchen.

This happened to be perfect timing because The Subject wasn't able to hold himself back any longer.

When The Restaurant Manager was back in his kitchen, Pepper reached across the table and affectionately touched The Subject's hand. He twitched slightly at the contact, but Pepper held strong and nodded at the entrees while saying, "This looks good, doesn't it?"

It was Veal Parmesan.

Pepper softly squeezed his hand and giggled. That was that. The Subject was off to the races.

After Pepper squeezed his hand, The Subject emitted a guttural noise as if he was simultaneously clearing his throat and lifting a weighty object. He used his free hand to grab Pepper's arm, stood up, and pulled her toward the exit, almost knocking over their table in the process.

Pepper was startled. She didn't understand what was taking place. She attempted to decelerate The Subject with a series of *waits* and *hold ons* and by mentioning that they hadn't yet eaten their entrees, but The Subject wasn't listening.

He had only one thing in mind.

One goal.

And he would achieve that goal no matter what.

#1 asked if it'd be wise to pacify The Subject. He knew I could do so easily with the two-way communicator. I stated that his plan was idiotic. Under no circumstance would we interfere with the test.

That was non-negotiable.

The Subject pulled Pepper outside and began groping her. He was extremely aggressive. No self-control whatsoever. I was a bit concerned since he was doing so out in the open. It was late and not another living soul roamed the quiet street, but still, one can never predict what or whom may pop up.

Fortunately, no one came around.

The Subject clawed at Pepper's dress, trying to rip it off her sylphlike body. Pepper squirmed and kicked, doing her best to put a stop to the ferociousness.

She even tried convincing The Subject that if he slowed down they could continue the date. She kept telling him, "That's enough! Let's go back and eat!"

When that didn't work Pepper screamed, "You can't do this!"

The Subject didn't surrender.

Pepper did all she could to wrestle free but The Subject's grip tightened around her body, like a predatory anaconda. The Subject then tore one of Pepper's shoulder straps off her dress.

This is when Pepper's statements went from firm to faltering.

Her voice shook as she said that somebody might see them in action. The Subject still did not surrender.

The Subject moved to unhook his belt buckle, but this gave him problems. Given that I'm the one who customarily dresses him, The Subject wasn't exactly swift or smooth with the unfastening.

Distracted by the sudden nuisance, The Subject briefly released Pepper to work on removing his pants. All it took was that split second.

Pepper took advantage and launched into a full sprint. She dashed as fast as she could. The Subject gave chase. #1 put the mobile laboratory in drive and followed.

There was a second or two when Pepper seemed as if she might escape. But that moment came and went as soon as she, for some inexplicable reason, turned into an alleyway. Like most alleyways, this one turned out to be a dead end.

Pepper balled her eyes out when realizing she was stuck with no exit.

I was unable to see the tears given the darkness of the night. But I had no problems hearing the wailing. Oh yes. They were beyond roaring and bounced off the encircling, windowless buildings. They were so loud that I was sure someone would soon arrive to step in the middle of my test.

I told #1 to keep the mobile laboratory in drive, just in case he needed to move his foot to the gas pedal and speed away from the scene. I did not want our experiment to be tampered with. Or even ruined. But I also did not want to be arrested as an accessory to what was about to happen.

None of my concern was necessary.

No one got in the middle of my test.

No one showed up to help the screaming woman. Not even as The Subject savagely ripped off her dress like it was a piece of paper.

That was the moment her screams hit quite the high note.

But not the highest.

The highest note came when The Subject threw his date to the ground while tearing away her black thong and shoving his extremely erect penis inside her vagina. With all the struggling, and with his lack of real life experience, it took The Subject several attempts to penetrate. When he finally did Pepper bellowed like she was burnt by the fires of ninety torches.

The screaming only further motivated The Subject.

Much like he did to his silicone love doll, he hauled off and belted Pepper across the mouth. There was no restraint from The Subject. No awareness of the strength he possessed over Pepper. He was on a mission. And with his fist already bloody, using all of the velocity and power he could pull together, The Subject smashed Pepper's face three more times.

Thud! Thud! Thud!

The sound of Pepper nearly choking to death on her own blood made #1 throw up in the mobile laboratory.

Great, I thought, now *this* colleague can't stomach the experiment.

But it wasn't the time for me to focus on such matters.

After The Subject turned Pepper's shouting into garbled sobbing, he began using frenzied and debauched thrusting. The same type of thrusting he learned from working on his love doll. I've once heard the expression: "Fucks like a jack rabbit." That was the first thing that came to mind while watching The Subject. That is if the word *fucks* was replaced with *rape*, and if *jack rabbit* was replaced with *drug fueled ogre*.

The Subject pushed and pumped and stabbed, all without a balanced cadence. He snatched Pepper's hair, removing clumps from her scalp. He squeezed and scratched at her breasts until she squealed like a tortured pig.

And then, for only the second time since the beginning of my experiment, The Subject spoke. It was more like a half vocalization/half snarl. But the style didn't matter. He could've whispered and it still would've shocked me.

Once I got over the surprise and considered what had been said, I realized just how much The Subject's brain had absorbed the pornography.

It was a simple statement. But it revealed a much larger picture. Leading up to his climax The Subject told Pepper, "Get ready bitch, I'm going to hose you down."

I don't believe The Subject understood exactly what he was saying, seeing as he ejaculated inside of Pepper, but he still made the statement. This exhibited that he was not only influenced by the pornography, but had also become a completely changed individual.

One would imagine that following his climax The Subject would become calmer. This was not the case.

The moment after his climax is when his ferocity intensified.

The Subject screamed like never before when he ejaculated. He screamed louder, more animalistic than he ever did with the love doll. Perhaps the feel of real flesh provoked this reaction.

But that was just a build-up to the actual frenzy.

Once The Subject ejaculated, instead of quieting down and relaxing, he delivered the most hellacious beating I have ever witnessed. And I have seen quite a few. Hell, I've been a part of many.

There was a second or two in between The Subject's climax and his next punch where nothing happened. Almost as if he was recapturing his bearings.

There was some heavy wheezing, both by The Subject and Pepper. Pepper seemed to feel the worst was over.

Terminating all hope for a ceasefire, The Subject's next punch came down like a jackhammer. From the sound alone I could easily tell he had shattered many of Pepper's teeth. Then, before she had a chance to plead for her life, The Subject threw a flurry of lefts and rights.

All in very metrical and solid fashion. Left. Right. Left. Right. Left. Right. Over and over and over again.

The punches never lost steam. Each blow was just as vicious as the first one.

The Subject turned Pepper's face into a gruesome explosion of blood and brokenness. And even when she no longer had the power to squirm and fight for freedom, even when there was virtually no life left, The Subject refused to relent.

Like an irate adolescent pulling grass out of a wild field, The Subject refocused on Pepper's scalp and removed four more clumps of hair.

As this went on #1 pleaded with me to end the test. He implored me to stop The Subject's grisliness. I told him no and grabbed my stun gun, just in case he tried to make his own moves.

If #1 tried to stop my test, I would've had no problem stopping *him*.

Not to mention, I knew The Subject very well. I knew everything would all come to an end at the appropriate time.

And of course that appropriate time did arrive.

There was absolutely zero resistance left in Pepper. Not even a slight twitch. She was lying on the concrete with only random tufts of hair left in her scalp, barely breathing, when The Subject finally decided to stop. Perhaps he had become either physically or mentally tired. Or both.

The Subject leaned forward and stared at Pepper's crushed face. There was no emotion on his own. He then rose from a crouched position, using his date's mangled face to give himself a boost, and slowly dressed himself.

Once dressed, The Subject reached down and grabbed Pepper's wrist. He stood in that position for a while. He looked like a formerly lost child who had just located his annihilated mother.

It was time to go.

The test was complete.

I opened the sliding door of the mobile laboratory and told The Subject to enter vehicle. He complied and, just as he had done in the basement with his love doll, dragged Pepper's body the whole way.

When he got to the mobile laboratory, The Subject released Pepper's wrist and entered the vehicle. Rather than leave the data of my experiment, I loaded Pepper's body in the back next to The Subject.

It wasn't easy.

Moving a nearly lifeless body, or any body for that matter, is a difficult task. But I pulled it off.

I also grabbed the maroon dress as well as Pepper's torn thong.

I returned to the vehicle and slid the door shut.

Off we went.

#1 k-turned to head back in the right direction. I looked into the restaurant as we drove by and saw the table where The Subject and Pepper sat only moments earlier. The plates had been cleared.

NOTE #11

KAREN: *Why don't you think #1 jumped out of the car and made a run for it? Not necessarily to save Pepper, but just to escape.*

DR. RAVENSDALE: *That's idiotic. Why would anyone want to escape the greatness I created?*

KAREN: Well, I've actually spoken with your former colleague and...

DR. RAVENSDALE: You've spoken with him?

KAREN: Yes.

DR. RAVENSDALE: What'd he say?

KAREN: He said you brainwashed him.

DR. RAVENSDALE: He said I brainwashed him? That's complete nonsense. He was in awe of me. He wanted to be me. Why do you think he assisted me for so long? He knew I was creating something powerful. This is, this is crazy. It's just that he can't handle the current criticism and is trying to evade the negativity by saying he was brainwashed. It's bullshit. If everybody recognized the genius of this experiment #1 would be the first person in line to accept admiration.

KAREN: I'm not sure about that. He's currently receiving treatment at a psychiatric hospital.

DR. RAVENSDALE: The fact that he's a traitor is obviously weighing down on him.

The drive back to our laboratory was quiet.

#1 drove. I could feel that he had a million thoughts and questions running through his mind. But he knew better than to open his mouth.

He never even glanced in the rearview mirror to look at me or The Subject. He did however fretfully and frequently look at the side mirrors. He did this to see if any cops were in pursuit.

They weren't.

Not at that point.

The Subject was also very silent. He hadn't moved an inch since entering the vehicle. He remained as frozen as a statue. The expression on his face was blank.

He didn't look pleased, nor miserable, nor remorseful. He didn't even look tired. This surprised me since he had just raped and beat a woman nearly to death.

He just looked straight ahead.

Whether his eyes or his mind were focused on anything in particular was anybody's guess.

Then there was Pepper. She did move, although her movement was very slight. Her eyes were completely sealed. Her face was so swollen it looked like a crimson balloon made of stone. But her body did spasm at times. Her breathing was limited, but it did trickle out.

This left me with a decision to make.

The odds of her survival were beyond slim, but they were theoretically existent. There was no doubt her brain was permanently damaged, but whether or not it was damaged to where she couldn't identify me or The Subject was impossible to tell. So I did the only thing I felt was right.

I clamped my hand over her mouth and nose and I squeezed.

It wasn't difficult to cut Pepper's oxygen. She had absolutely no strength to fight.

Her body released a couple additional twitches. The ones closer to death more drastic than the others. But none of them ever came close to stopping me. Her spasms and jerks were so minor they didn't even draw the attention of #1.

Pepper ceased to exist within the matter of seconds.

***

The overall atmosphere became even darker when we arrived at the laboratory. The gloominess formed when #1 realized that the new burial hole in the backyard would need to be large enough for two.

He was already crestfallen as we carried Pepper's body into the house. Once he approached #2 and realized that his former colleague was dead as well, well, #1 really lost control.

It was the first time throughout the experiment that I considered eliminating #1. All I wanted was to think. I wanted to mull over the next moves in terms of cleaning and think about the amazing results of this test.

I should've been ecstatic.

The Subject had brilliantly blown the experiment wide open. He showed exactly what happens when one tries to date while only understanding a world of pornography.

It was a magnificent result and I should've been ecstatic. But I had to contend with #1's crying and shouting. Like a madman, he kept hollering about how he couldn't understand what happened. How he couldn't make sense of #2's death. How he should've "been there" for him.

I had to extinguish the blaze the best I could. I had to hit #1 with the perfect fusion of honesty and deception. I had to do so to keep him well-balanced and on my side.

"We had our issues and we didn't always see eye to eye," I told #1 while pointing at #2's corpse. "But this is an absolute tragedy. A damn shame."

I took a breath to let that statement sink in for #1. A statement that was a complete lie.

"But you know very well what happened here," I continued. "It was the attack. If only our colleague listened to me and took his time…I don't know…We can blame The Subject all we want, but he didn't know any better."

I paused once more.

"But listen to me," I carried on, moving closer to #1. "We are making progress here. I know this is difficult to think about right now, but we are on the verge of one of the most groundbreaking discoveries known to man. We must move forward. In my heart of hearts, I truly believe it would be a mistake to stop this experiment."

I grabbed #1's shoulder tightly and asked, "Right?"

#1 provided a small nod. I'll never forget that nod. It was the nod of a man who was exceedingly petrified. The nod of a man who didn't know which way to turn. The nod a man I had complete control over.

Or so I thought.

I must say, that thought felt nice.

Not only did it feel as if I had #1 in the palm of my hand, I also had The Subject in there as well, who, by the way, was being a real trooper about everything.

As soon as we returned to the laboratory, before #1 and I dragged Pepper's body inside, I unlocked the door to the basement and The Subject entered without a single word or a single tear.

He entered with his head held high and returned to his home like a conqueror.

Upon returning to the basement, The Subject moved slowly yet confidently to his mattress, which laid without a frame on the floor, got under the covers in somewhat of a childlike manner, and fell asleep almost instantly. He didn't even need an injection.

I gave him one anyway. Just for good measure.

With The Subject asleep, after I finally removed the shell-shocked #1 from the dead body of #2, we went out to the mobile laboratory to retrieve Pepper's corpse.

Straight to the backyard with it!

The work was done during the late evening hours. Not that it mattered. We were in total isolation. But it still felt good to perform these acts under the moonlight. It felt safe.

We dropped Pepper's body in the backyard and retrieved #2. His stench was already beginning to emerge, so it was best to get him under ground as soon as possible.

While #1 watched the bodies, I went to the garage and grabbed the shovel left by previous owners. The previous owners only left one shovel, so #1 and I had to switch off with the digging.

Kind of.

After a while I wound up taking over the whole operation and digging by myself. #1 couldn't stop crying and didn't have the power to handle the assignment. It was embarrassing. But I was in no mood to quarrel, so I just took it upon myself to get the job done.

It was no easy task. The work was backbreaking. It took me a little over an hour to get deep enough into the earth's surface. There's no way I made it six feet, but I went far and wide enough to fit both #2 and Pepper. I then re-shoveled the dirt on the bodies to finish the job.

I was wiped.

Completely worn out.

It had been a long day.

But after the burial, I still took the opportunity to gaze up at the stunning May sky. It was a cloudless evening. The constellations were spectacular. Seeing the stars reminded me of my importance. Breathing and appreciating the air helped me understand the significance of my experiment. It helped me understand how I will influence society's outlook in years to come.

I felt like a very lucky man.

I tried getting #1's attention. I wanted to share with him my happiness. But he was standing next the new burial site, gone in his own world.

Trembling and whimpering like a lost boy, he existed in a much smaller world. A world I refused to accept.

I returned to the laboratory, leaving the shovel in the backyard, not caring if #1 followed. Although he eventually did.

I heard the back door lock about three minutes after I entered. I guess #1 took that time to continue being infantile.

Not bothering myself with that nonsense, I turned on the monitors and watched the feed to the basement. The Subject was still in bed. His eyes were closed. His feet were crossed and his fingers were intertwined behind his head. I can't be entirely certain about this, but I believe he also had a small smirk on his face.

I knew The Subject was safe and sound.

I went off to my room without telling #1 to watch the monitors.

I didn't even bother taking a shower to wash off the dirt and blood. I didn't care about the grime. I was too satisfied with the experiment to worry about cleanliness.

Off to bed I went, where I found myself smirking as well. I eventually nodded off to the sounds of #1 crying.

Test #3 – Building Thick Skin

Perhaps it would've been wise of me to begin my experiment with this test. I probably should've started the entire process by using it on #1 and #2.

Could've, should've, would've. Too late.

At that point, #2 was decomposing in the backyard. And #1 was far gone. Too far gone to even understand anything about tough skin.

With the results of Test #2, results I consider to be trailblazing, #1 became glum. Irksomely glum. It was like I had another job just getting him out of bed in the morning. Maddening.

I already had enough on my plate. And if getting him out of bed was difficult, imagine what it was like making him do *his* job.

Just getting him to watch the monitors was enough to test my patience.

Everything should've been moving smoothly. The experiment should've been riding on easy street. I should've had no burdens whatsoever. But that wasn't the case.

#1's disgraceful ways were evidence that I could no longer depend on him.

This was partially fine since I had grown accustomed to doing all the major work myself.

But I didn't want to fire #1.

Back to my old reasoning, he knew too much and I wanted to keep him close. I was also hoping against hope that he would snap out of his funk and return to being somewhat of a reliable colleague.

Although I knew this to be a long shot.

Following the burial of #2 and Pepper, #1 displayed no sign of strength.

That's why I knew Test #3 would have zero positive effect on him.

But I didn't care about that. I didn't care how #2 felt. His feelings had nothing to do with my ambition.

What I cared about was the mental and physical reactions of The Subject. That was the beginning, middle, and end for me.

***

Turning my attention back The Subject, back to what I was saying earlier; yes, perhaps it would've been wise to begin my experiment with this test.

The Subject had exhibited in many ways that he was far from feeble.

The Subject proved to be quite strong when it came to his ability to physically dominate.

But this was only true in situations where he was the strongest person in the room. Situations where there was no chance of him being bullied into a corner.

He was overpowering people like The Library Manager, The Older Woman, #2, and Pepper. None of these folks were tough enough to challenge The Subject. None of them possessed the fortitude to push The Subject and see if he could brave the heat.

This inspired me to conduct Test #3.

I wanted to see if The Subject had the ability to bear the brunt when provoked by a real opponent. If not, I wanted to see if he had the determination to build thicker skin.

Physical durability was not my main priority with this test. The Subject had already demonstrated that he could take a hit from my stun gun, which was no easy feat.

Don't get me wrong, there were moments where I wanted to see if The Subject could take *more* physical punishment.

The thought briefly crossed my mind to hire a group of heavy hitters to come through for three months and wail on The Subject for hours at a time. Just beat the bloody hell out of him.

It would've been interesting to see those results. But it would not have been consistent with my experiment as a whole. The driving force of my experiment was always linked with the psyche, particularly in relation to technology. All that was accomplished derived from everything The Subject had seen on his electronic devices.

It was imperative for me to remain on that course with this test.

***

I believe I wrote earlier that my comprehension of the internet enhanced due to my experiment. By watching The Subject cruise various sites, and by having to do so myself in order to maintain familiarity, I was able to learn many things about the land of interconnectivity.

I learned about the high volume of accessible pornography. I also discovered how easy it is for anyone to get nearly anything they could ever desire.

Almost any item is purchasable thanks to the internet. There's Amazon, EBay, Craigslist. And then there are other sites. Sites that are far shadier. Including the page where I bought my Glock 20/10mm pistol, which was utilized in this test.

But more on that later.

The thing I learned most about was the level of hate people have for humanity. People hate other people. This is easy to see by reading almost any message board on most websites.

No matter what someone posts, no matter if the one writing the initial message is making complete sense, there will be an abundance of others castigating the original poster.

On occasion, posters are targeted by one or more of the malicious antagonists and the criticizing develops into online bullying.

I knew nothing about these activities prior to my research. Apparently it is somewhat of a widespread predicament in certain areas, particularly with kids in High School, and especially with teenaged homosexuals.

As I had come to learn, after spending all day with one another at school, many students rush home and use the internet to continue their association. A lot of kids use it to directly tease others. Some go farther and create entire pages, sites of pure maliciousness, to publically humiliate another classmate.

Again, ordinarily the one being shamed is homosexual. And many times, after suffering much maltreatment and mortification in the online presence of their peers, the homosexual student commits suicide.

I found all of this to be fascinating.

It was a completely different world to me.

I was tormented as a youth. But the bullying was carried out during school hours and always involved bodily harm as opposed to mental torture, which is exactly what online bullying exemplifies.

Mental torture.

From what I was able to learn during my research, I found that nowadays very little victimization occurs at school. However, when the children arrive home, they find it virtually impossible to avoid the internet, which of course is where the bullying kicks into gear.

Once I learned this, I knew that I had my motivation for Test #3.

The big question for me was: could The Subject take others ridiculing his appearance and behavior?

I was unsure. I didn't know if The Subject could stand up to a bombardment of invectives. I didn't know if he had that type of strength.

I could've simply done the bullying myself. I could've sat upstairs and created a fake online personality to mock The Subject. I did that to some extent for the job rejections during Test #1.

But doing so didn't feel right on this go around. Too manufactured. I needed something more genuine. I needed the harrying to spring from a stranger.

The key to any test of this nature, as well as to the discovery of anything societally significant, is authenticity. For this test to be realistic, it was essential for me to acquire the proper ingredient. I needed someone around the same age as The Subject. And I needed this person to be as clever as he was rancorous.

The first step to this discovery was finding all the nearby high schools. None of the institutes were round the corner, given the seclusion of my laboratory, but I could still complete the job thanks to my vehicle and proper devotion.

There were four high schools within a drivable distance. The closest being fifty-seven minutes away. The furthest was two hours and twenty-three minutes away. I intended on visited each and every one.

And that's exactly what I did.

Begrudgingly bringing with me a sullen #1, who wasn't speaking much at that point, I spent months driving out time and again to the first three school without much success. I always set out early to be around for the various outdoor gym classes throughout the day. I did this so I could monitor the children in action.

I'm aware of how strange this sounds. I also understand that the creepiness of my process, if noticed by some outside unit, could have irreparably jeopardized my experiment.

But much to my delight, I was never seen by a student, or a teacher, or any other authoritative individual, so I never aroused any suspicion. This kind of amazed me.

Granted, I never left the vehicle and I always monitored the students through my binoculars, but I was still stunned that I was detected by no one.

***

The first eleven weeks of my search were uneventful.

I had monitored the first three schools for hours, searching every inch of those playgrounds for a gargantuan brute who could talk a lot of trash and have the muscularity to back it up.

I needed a big bully.

But that type wasn't present at those first three schools.

It was peculiar.

There were surely a lot of team activities, I'll tell you that. Teachers helping students. Students helping other students. It was all very baffling. Everyone seemed to be in a pleasant mood. It was nothing like when I was in secondary school. Nothing like when I was being flattened almost every single day.

I was beginning to think that I was either coming up empty on this test, or, to get a closer look, I would have to dig deeper and find a way into these schools as a worker. A maintenance man perhaps.

I was not a fan of either route. Particularly the latter. I felt my face would become too visible and that would've harmed my experiment.

It thankfully didn't come to that.

It was week twelve of my search when I arrived at the fourth school and finally located the ideal candidate.

The candidate was a monster. He was unquestionably mature for his junior class, at least when it came to his physical appearance. He was 6'3" and I estimated him to be roughly 16 stone. Or roughly 225 pounds.

A big boy.

And although I never stuck around past his gym class, I could tell he was a footballer. Helmut and shoulder pads type. Not shin guards and headers.

Perfect.

He was a fine looking boy as well. Sharp features. Wavy blonde hair. Blue eyes. A real standout. The young girls loved him. This love gave him great confidence. Another exceptional feature that I figured would come in handy.

Along with his build and poise came the aptitude to bully the visibly weaker students. When I saw this I figured he most likely terrorized throughout the rest of the school day, as well as when he arrived home and sat in front of his computer.

Doubly perfect. An ideal menace.

He shoved and punched the other students during his gym classes. He did this often and jubilantly so, like it was his treasured occupation. Some kids tried running away from The Bully. Others cowered in fear right in front of him, as if they were trying to magically vanish.

I watched all of this and felt my excitement raise. The Bully had the power to not only physically dominate but mentally torment as well.

I saw it all.

The Bully ridiculing the weight of an obese student.

The Bully poking fun at the disfigurement of another.

The Bully criticizing a deprived student for his tattered clothing.

The Bully did all of this with impunity.

By the spirited tousling of The Bully's hair and the athletic slapping of his bottom, I could tell his gym teacher was also his coach at school. I assumed he was the football coach and did not want one of his players getting in trouble. So he let The Bully roam free and intimidate like an unpitying totalitarian.

What a show!

The more I watched The Bully the more I wanted him. The desire was great and I knew I needed to act fast.

But I also understood that excessive impetuosity could cause chaos. I required a quick plan but also a calculated plan so as not lose or get caught acquiring The Bully.

There was also the need for additional preparation with The Subject.

Thus, knowing where and what I needed to do to find The Bully, I had the small window to shift focus and begin organizing The Subject's mind.

The preparation was simple.

I showed The Subject websites where online posters unremittingly harassed one another. I made him sit for many hours in front of the computer, reading the bitterness. I remained in the basement and stood over his shoulder as he absorbed it all. Pages and pages of malice.

When asking The Subject if he understood what was happening, he simply nodded and kept scrolling and reading.

I asked him, "Are you sure you understand? You see what's happening here? This group has ganged up to insult this individual because he's gay. Do you understand?"

Once again he nodded.

I continued: "They feel this person is different and they don't like different people, so they're doing everything they can to hurt him and make him feel bad about himself. The fact that they can do so anonymously provides them with even more power. They are in a safe zone. They can say anything."

Another nod.

"Look, look over here," I said, pointing to another feed on the screen. "This video is honoring Dr. Martin Luther King. Do you know who that is?"

The Subject stared at the screen without responding.

"He was a very significant person in history, particularly with leading the 1960's civil rights movement in America. But some of these people on the boards dislike African Americans, you see. That's why they're using such words as, *monkey* and *nigger*."

The Subject chewed his bottom lip.

"Fearing that they might be fired, beaten, or ostracized, these commenters can't openly display their indignation anywhere else but on these message boards, and perhaps in private get-togethers. So when they have the opportunity to do so, as they do online, they let their true selves soar, even though they're using aliases."

I couldn't tell if The Subject was fully understanding my statements. I was talking a lot. More than I ever spoke in one sitting.

I wouldn't say that I was treating The Subject like an equal. But he had proven himself up to that point and earned the right to be educated. He had shown that he was at least marginally perceptive and worthy of an exchange.

But I still couldn't tell if he was fully hearing me. This probably had more to do with how absorbed he became with all the online hatred.

He particularly enjoyed the boards where collections of posters ganged up on one person. This was wonderful. This is where I wanted his focus.

Even if he wasn't totally comprehending my explanations, The Subject was heading in the right direction. And he was becoming highly enthusiastic.

I suppose I felt somewhat guilty about my design.

In the matter of days, I planned to flip the mood on The Subject. Although he wasn't typing and contributing to the online animosity, I could tell he was siding with the bullies. He enjoyed their attack on the weak.

I planned for that to change once I integrated The Bully into the test.

But I didn't want to bother The Subject with that alteration just yet. There was still more ground to cover.

I incorporated a larger dose of reality for The Subject. I played from him several videos involving online bullying, starting with the calmer ones, then advancing to the more intense.

I started with world news stories covering the dangers and damages associated with cyberbullying. Given that the news can only show so much graphic content, the videos weren't exactly hard-hitting. But it set the tone.

I then advanced to online documentaries about school shootings. The type of shootings that began due to ill-treatment. I located hours of coverage and offered that footage to The Subject.

Footage of bullying. Footage of shootings. Testimonials from weeping parents who lost children. Declarations from students who survived the violence. It was all very informative.

I then moved onto something I called The Showstopper.

Without much effort I was able to locate a video of a high school student – former, I should say – delivering quite the potent message. The student's skin was very pale. His hair was sandy blonde. His eyes would've been crystal blue if they weren't masked by tears and inflammation.

He was also a homosexual.

Nearly drowning in his own despondency, whimpering directly into his camera, The Student spoke on how badly he was bullied by his classmates. He stated that on numerous occasions he attempted to, "Pray himself straight." But no matter how hard he tried, he eventually discovered that there was nothing he could do to convert himself.

Due to his natural attractions and inability to change, the students at his Catholic school made his life a living hell. Name-calling and thrashings were common.

The last straw broke when a classmate created a website where others could make fun of The Student. The photo on the page was a picture of The Student with his mouth open. Someone manipulated the photo to where a penis approached The Student's mouth. It was done in a very uncomplimentary manner.

The video of The Student explaining these details was twelve minutes and forty-four seconds long. Most of the video involved him talking about how difficult his life had become and how his despair was caused by the insensitivity of others.

Then, with twelve seconds left until the end of the video, The Student put a pistol to his head and pulled the trigger.

It shocked me.

My body jumped a bit.

The Subject didn't move.

Not at first.

He just watched as the video ended and the screen went black. Following about twenty seconds of staring at the black screen, The Subject grabbed the mouse, located the part where The Student pulled the trigger, and replayed that section.

The Subject replayed again and again.

I thought about the video as a whole once my initial shock was gone. Not so much about the shooting. More about who stopped the recording.

It must've been a friend of The Student. I bet the friend didn't think it would go down the way it did. But once the deed was done, I suppose that friend felt he had no other choice but to fulfill The Student's last wish and upload the video.

I was surprised the video still existed online. Bots usually remove such content once discovered.

I kept thinking about this stuff.

Not The Subject. All he focused on was replaying those final twelve seconds.

***

With The Subject hooked on all forms of online bullying, I moved on to the next part of Test #3. The Acquisition. I needed The Bully! But remaining smart was also a priority.

I rented a small family car using one of my fake identifications and the credit card under that name. I didn't want my mobile laboratory discovered if things went sideways. Too much sensitive material inside.

Day after day I set out to observe the gym class at the fourth school. I needed to be 100% certain that The Bully was the right choice. That he was my guy. It wasn't enough watching him in action on only a few occasions. I needed to see him frequently. I needed to make sure he wasn't someone who could bully one day only to be bullied the next.

I'm glad I checked.

Not because The Bully was tormented on another day. Absolutely not. I'm glad I checked because I was able to see just how correct I was about his supremacy.

The more I observed The Bully during those gym classes, the more nasty and devious he became. It was almost as if he knew he had an audience and wanted to showcase his talents.

He was an absolute beast.

I knew if there was anyone who could test The Subject, it would be The Bully.

The decision was made.

The Bully would become a part of my experiment. All that was left was getting him back to my laboratory.

I required two things to obtain The Bully. One: the ability to focus. Concentration would provide me the mindset to tail The Bully and realize the correct moment for capture. Two: A syringe full of Butorphanol. The latter was less complicated.

The moment I knew The Bully was right for my experiment, I loaded a clean syringe back at the laboratory and stashed it in the glove compartment of my rental.

It was a must to be prepared at all times.

I then decided to tail The Bully after he left school. That was my plan. Simple enough in theory.

But finding his vehicle was not exactly easy. It's not like I could've entered the school and asked the principle for the information, could I? There was also the chance of The Bully not being of proper age to operate a vehicle.

This would've been most unfortunate.

Luckily it wasn't the case.

One day after a gym class, instead of accompanying the rest of the students back to school, The Bully darted off in a different direction. He made his way toward the parking lot and over to what turned out to be his vehicle – a brand new mustang. All black with strikingly polished hubcaps.

The Bully retrieved something from his back seat while I retrieved a valuable piece of ammo: the license plate information.

I no longer had the tricky task of trying to spot The Bully when the final bell rang and students rushed out like a mad parade. One would imagine it would be effortless to spot a 6'3" teenager in the midst of significantly smaller students. But it wasn't. Those damn kids are so speedy. They dash in so many directions. It's really difficult to keep track.

That was no longer a problem.

Not only did I know The Bully's form from top to bottom, I also knew the vehicle he drove. All I needed now was the best time and place to inject him.

The fewer witnesses the better.

The Bully made the injection process complicated.

Getting him alone was the most difficult part. We went from the school parking lot to his friend's home the first three times I followed him. At his friend's house was a collection of seven teenagers, including The Bully, all lounging on the front porch smoking and playing beer pong.

They'd occasionally wrestle one another.

Although they were all well-proportioned, The Bully was the largest of the group. I was happy to see this since it verified my decision.

But all the mucking about left me with no opening to do what was required.

Following the drinking and wrestling, The Bully would head home, just as the sun began its descent and, almost always, he and his parents would pull into the drive at the same time. The Bully had it all timed out. Further evidence that he also had a functioning brain. This would be beneficial when I needed him to devise insults against The Subject.

But The Bully's routine was so well orchestrated it had me worrying that we wouldn't get a moment alone. I began contemplating an alternative strategy, just in case a solo opportunity never materialized. I envisioned a scheme that involved the anesthetizing of either his friends or his entire family.

I ultimately didn't have to go that route.

I was pleasantly surprised on my fourth day of tailing when, after leaving his school's parking lot, The Bully took a different route and drove directly home.

This was my moment.

If I didn't strike at that point I might not have gotten another chance. Plus, I had spent so much time tracking The Bully that I was slightly neglecting The Subject. I didn't like this.

#1 was at the laboratory, and, when it came to the short-term, his mind was technically sound enough to handle any complications. But I still wasn't comfortable with that arrangement. #1 was too fragile. He had been crying a lot those days. It wasn't overly vexatious. He usually did it at night while alone in his room. But it was constant. And it showed me that the more time I spent away from the laboratory the greater the chance of something bad happening.

The time had come for me to act fast.

NOTE #12

KAREN: *Don't you think this was #1's way of saying he needed help? If not from you then from an outside entity.*

DR. RAVENSDALE: *How could you think I would include an outside entity to help #1?*

KAREN: *Because he was in desperate need of it. As a man who once saved lives I'm sure you could understand that.*

DR. RAVENSDALE: *Don't treat me like a child. My years at the hospital were entirely different than my years with my experiment. So don't compare the two. Secondly, I couldn't have cared less about #1 needing help. He was nothing more than another tool in my laboratory.*

The Bully pulled into his drive, a piece of paved asphalt supporting neither of his parents' vehicles. Brilliant.

If my tracking had showed me anything it was that I had approximately four hours to make the grab. Plenty of time if I operated proficiently.

I watched as The Bully made his way past the handicap ramp leading to his front door, unlocked the front door and entered his house. Understanding that very few people, particularly those in his age group, ever think something out of the ordinary might occur, I had a feeling he wouldn't lock up.

Thirty minutes later I discovered I was correct.

I waited the thirty minutes in order let The Bully settle in and get comfortable. I then excited my rental car, which I parked a block away, strolled up to the front steps and entered without anxiety.

I immediately noticed two things upon entering the house. First was the blasting music coming from upstairs, from what I assumed was The Bully's room. The second thing I noticed was the small area to the left of the entrance foyer.

I looked inside and saw an old lady resting in a hospital bed. A Drive Medical electric bed, to be exact. State of the art.

I had to assume she was The Bully's grandmother. She was obviously in poor health and was being looked after by her family.

Next to her bed was a power wheelchair. An additional Drive Medical device. The Sunfire Gladiator. Yet another fine piece of machinery. This family certainly had money. If I was destitute I might've considered holding The Bully for ransom.

The old lady was out cold. There were no signs she'd wake up in the near future. Or at all, for that matter. So nothing to worry about on that front.

I climbed the steps and advanced toward the music.

I probably moved slower than necessary seeing as there was no way The Bully could hear me. But better safe than sorry.

As I continued rising, I slid my hand over the mechanical stairlift rail attached to the wall. A rail that could be used by the grandmother to get from the first floor to the second, and vice versa. While feeling the lift, I used my other hand to remove the syringe from the right pocket of my jacket.

The music grew louder the closer I inched to The Bully's bedroom. I couldn't exactly identify the type of composition. All I can say is that it seemed to combine a number of booming sounds that made my flesh pulsate.

My first thought: The Bully was bound to get noise-induced hearing loss if he continued listening to music at that volume. My second thought: thank goodness he listened at that volume. He'd never hear me coming.

As for vision, The Bully would only see me coming if he was facing the entry. He wasn't. I discovered this as I lightly pushed open his bedroom door to make my move.

Entering the room I saw The Bully in front of his computer. He was typing away and laughing at his own comment. I knew it was a hateful message when he cackled once more and gave his monitor the middle finger.

I didn't notice anything else in his bedroom. I remained focused on my target. I crept closer while preparing myself to jam the needle into The Bully's neck.

The music was roaring. The entire room felt like it was vibrating. Yet my heart rate was steady.

There was only one instant when my heart jumped. This was right before I injected The Bully. I'm not sure if he simply felt my presence or caught a glimpse of me in the reflection of his monitor, but when he turned around I experienced a flash of apprehension.

But being a professional, I did not let this deter me. I stuck the needle into The Bully's neck at great speed. I'll never forget the look on his face. Or looks, I should say.

When The Bully first saw me he expressed fear mixed with surprise. But when he felt the needle slide into his neck his mood transformed to fear mixed with the panic of death. As a man who loves to study human behavior, to me, it was quite the epic conversion. One I will never forget.

Something else I won't forget was the battle between myself and The Bully.

In one fluid motion he tore the empty syringe from his neck and jumped out of his computer chair, lunging at me. But by then it was too late. The Butorphanol was coursing its way through his bloodstream.

But I will say this, in the brief moment before the drug clutched The Bully, I was able to see and feel his power. He had his one hand on my shoulder with the other wrapped around my throat. His thumb pressed firmly above the laryngeal prominence.

In that moment I thought that I might have botched the job. I had been administering so many drugs to The Subject that I thought I might have accidently switched needles and given The Bully a shot of Pentedrone. That's how powerful he was.

But I knew I had it right when his grip finally relaxed and his thumb eased off my throat.

Next came the wobbling.

The Bully began to rock back and forth as the Butorphanol did its job. He looked like a concerned drunkard unpleasantly reaching his limit. Then came the look in The Bully's eyes. A wonderful look. A look that exhibited two questions: *What did you give me/What is happening to me?*

Then…lights out.

As he fell I pushed The Bully back in the direction of his computer chair, which had providentially spun with him as he rose to attack. He dropped perfectly into the chair and vanished into the land of unconsciousness.

I felt lucky to have The Bully fall in that fashion. He was rather large. Dragging him to the staircase would've taken much time and effort.

Minus that burden, I wheeled The Bully with ease to the top of the steps and moved his body onto the mechanical stairlift.

I let the stairlift handle the heavy work as I triggered its descent and walked down the steps simply holding The Bully in place. Who needs human colleagues after all?

Once we arrived at first floor I activated the Grandmother's wheel chair, transferred The Bully, and wheeled him down the outside ramp and out to my rental car.

I thought momentarily about the wheelchair after loading The Bully into the front seat. I thought about returning it to the Grandmother's room. Not because I was worried about her ability to move, but because I did not want to raise any suspicion. But then I realized that I was abducting a family member, which was something they would surely notice. So I figured there was no point in returning the chair.

Plus, it would come in handy with transporting The Bully from the car to my laboratory.

Using all the energy I saved from not carrying The Bully, I lifted the heavy machine and stuffed it into my backseat.

Another phase complete.

I found myself becoming somewhat aggravated when returning to the laboratory. Getting The Bully inside wasn't the easiest chore, even with the assistance of the wheelchair.

It was that labor mixed with #1 becoming nothing more than dead weight that set me off. Not only was he too depressed to help bring The Bully to the basement, he was too miserable to do anything at all, including bathing himself. His attitude infuriated me.

Breakthroughs with the experiment were being continuously made and he was acting as if he had been castrated. I wasn't having it.

When I entered with The Bully, I took one look around before setting my sights on #1, who was curled up on the couch like a slothful vagrant, and began shouting about the state of the laboratory. It was beyond filthy.

I demanded that #1 get off the couch and begin scrubbing. If he wouldn't assist with the heavy lifting he would sure as hell be useful in a janitorial sense.

Most of the untidiness was my fault, but that wasn't the point. I was the real worker. I was the professional putting in time for the experiment. I wasn't the unshaven one bumming around in begrimed clothing, crying about a body buried out back.

And yes, yes, yes. I realize I was partially responsible for that body, for all those bodies in fact, but that doesn't mean I lack emotion. It just means that I am far more intellectual than sensitive! Far more occupationally composed!

If a few people had to forfeit their lives for the sake of experimental ascertainment, then so be it. I was fine with those deaths because I knew they would lead to brilliance.

Think about it; this world is much bigger than an old woman, a library manager, a whore and a shoddy colleague.

I know the actual magnitude of this place! You know how I know? Because I live in the real world! I live in a world where tough decisions are made every day. Where difficult choices are made by those who can actually handle the obligation. By those who don't allow the erroneous opinions of others to block the path of innovation. That was me. That was my role as I led the experiment. And that's why I was so harsh with #1.

In hindsight, perhaps I shouldn't have been so rash. Not because he didn't deserve it. And not because I was concerned about his mental fragility. Because, in a way, it was his cleaning sessions that basically put me in this cell.

But I don't want to get into that right now. We still have ground to cover. I'll become too furious and won't be able to focus.

While lowering The Bully down to the basement, step by step, I heard #1 finally get off the couch and begin cleaning.

"Good," I said to myself. "Now I can do some real work."

After I got The Bully down to the basement I looked up to see The Subject in his chair. He was leaning toward his computer. There was only about a ten inches of space between his face and the monitor.

He was watching the same video I had showed him nearly a week earlier. The one of the student committing suicide.

Well, The Subject wasn't doing only that.

He was alternating. Clicking and switching back and forth between the suicide video and various online message boards. When I moved closer I saw that The Subject was examining a page that jubilantly detailed the effects, and also encouraged the further use, of cyberbullying.

A poster shared in one message a link to someone's Facebook page. Underneath the link the poster wrote: "This kid is in my class and he's the only spic there. He smells like shit and he's dumber as fuck. U all hit him up until he hurts himself or quits school."

Beneath the poster's comment were both a thumbs up and a thumbs down button. The number 57 was next to the thumbs up icon. Next to the thumbs down icon was the number 0.

When The Subject finished reading the message he released two grunting laughs, then moved the mouse until the cursor was over the thumbs up icon and clicked.

The Subject was number 58.

What progress!

I knew this test would become quite thought-provoking once The Bully was awake.

I didn't bother leaving the basement. I could've went upstairs and used the monitors to watch everything, but no. There was something holding me down there. I wanted to be close. At least until everything was underway.

I let The Subject remain in his world of internet tormenters as I kept close to The Bully. I stood over him. Watched as he continued to sleep and regularly suck in air. I imagined the type of young cheerleader he probably dated. I imagined the type of laughs him and his friend had while being popular in the midst of parties. I went on imagining things of this nature for a while.

Then The Bully came around

It was a slow process at first.

He woke up as if he was coming out of a coma. This was due to the quantity of Butorphanol I injected.

Mind unsteady, eyes cloudy, mouth trickling and muttering, The Bully had no idea about his current state. He might not have even known who he was.

The Bully's haziness developed into confusion which then transformed into panic. The rubberiness that the drug provided his body evaporated and he became extremely stiff right before he started struggling and showcasing his anger.

Anticipating such a reaction, I had chained The Bully tightly to his chair prior to him waking. No one enjoys being drugged against their will and waking up in an unfamiliar area. So it was a must to take the necessary precautions.

When The Bully's tough guy act dissolved and he realized that he was detained and under my control, his cries rang out like a newborn frightened of their peculiar world. The howls were explosive.

I looked at The Subject to see if he was distracted by such an eruption. He wasn't. He had moved even closer to his monitor.

Me?

I wasn't distracted. Not in the slightest.

But I was a bit repulsed by the cries. I understand the whole situation was shocking to The Bully, but I still expected him to be tougher. I found his tears rather embarrassing. They kind of made me laugh, which I did openly, right in front of The Bully's face.

My laughter instigated more tears and senseless squirming.

I explained to The Bully that I didn't *want* to hurt him. I chose my words deliberately, speaking in a way that said he was getting on my nerves and, if he continued, I would have no other choice but to cause him harm.

This slightly did the trick.

I informed The Bully of the details once he fell silent. I told him that he was participating in a revolutionary experiment. I told him the he should feel privileged to be part of such a marvelous process.

This is when he began whimpering out all of the *What's going on here-s*, the *Where am I-s*, the *Why me-s* and the *What're are you going to do to me-s*.

Although I knew it was risky, I figured honesty would help The Bully concentrate. I told him that I required his strength and brutishness to torture The Subject.

When The Bully acted confused, I informed him that I had been watching his every move. I told him that I knew about his talents. His knack at making the lives of others exceedingly agonizing. I told him he no longer had to hide his true self.

The Bully shook his head and whined that I was mistaken. I smacked him cruelly across the face, believing the blow would snap him out of his funk. It didn't work. It only made him cry more.

When I smacked The Bully, out of my peripheral, I noticed The Subject turn in our direction and emit a hoarse laugh.

Not the result I expected. But one I gladly accepted.

As The Bully continued to cry and bellow about his desire to return home, and as The Subject continued to devour the world of cyberbullying, I began arranging the rest of my experiment.

It wasn't much.

Along with a fresh syringe of Butorphanol, I brought down to the basement two laptops and set them back to back, similar to the game of Battleship. Off to the side of the computers, within reaching distance, I positioned a small round end table. On the table I placed the 10mm pistol that I purchased online. I then flicked the switch that initiated the pistol's outer layer, a device I had personally built and attached to the weapon. It was an electronic shell perfectly molded over the pistol that released a low but painful shock whenever touched.

It wasn't difficult to build the shell. All I needed was a few supplies and a working knowledge of electric current. Knowledge I most certainly possessed.

I made sure the shell was not in the way of the pistol's trigger.

With everything arranged, I ushered The Subject to The Battle Station and told him it was his new workspace. He agreed without speaking. He didn't even nod. He just stared at me briefly then looked at his new laptop, awaiting further instructions.

Loud enough for both of them to hear, not wanting to repeat myself, I explained that The Bully would be using the other laptop to type messages directly to The Subject. I then stated that The Bully would be very cruel in order to see how The Subject managed the mistreatment.

I then walked over to The Bully with a purpose. His crying had reduced. But his eyes still conveyed consternation.

I grabbed him intensely by his chin and brought my face close to his. His breath smelled ancient, as if his personal hygiene was a thing of disremembered past. I leaned in even more and whispered,

"You listen to me boy, now's the time to buck up. Just imagine that this is the big game. Fourth quarter. You need to do what you do best. Okay?"

"Okay, but..." The Bully stuttered. "I don't know...I don't know what you want me to do... Please don't make me do anything sexual. Please sir, I..."

"*Sexual?*" I interrupted, feeling my choler escalate. It was as if he didn't listen to my speech. This made me want to hit him with additional fright.

"What'd you think is happening here? Do you think he's going to rape you?" I asked this while pointing at The Subject.

The Bully began crying again.

"Do you think *I'm* going to rape you?" I let this question dangle in the air for a moment. I wanted the image to expand and take form and terrify The Bully.

It worked.

The Bully wept harder than ever before and repeatedly muttered the word *please*. If it all wasn't so exhilarating it would've been pathetic.

I put my hand on his shoulder and said, "Nothing like that will happen here. Nothing bad will happen to you at all... if you do exactly what I need you to do."

The student quieted down and did his best to straighten his body.

"I told you that I've been watching you," I continued. "I've seen the way you treat other students. Other *weaker* students. You make their lives awful."

"No! No I don't!" The Bully fired back. "I'm not that kind of..."

"Stop it! I know exactly what you are! That's why you're here. I need you to utilize those bullying skills and make his life a living hell." I pointed once more to The Subject. "Things will become unpleasant if you do not accept this assignment. Do you understand?"

I stuck The Bully with the fresh needle before he had the chance to answer, putting him to sleep.

I was back upstairs in front of the monitors by the time The Bully awoke.

#1 was back on the couch taking a break from the housework. Being annoyingly depressed.

What a bastard.

I should've known better.

I should've taken the time right then and there to put him in the ground next to #2. But how could I have known what would take place? I couldn't see the approaching madness. All I could see was optimism. All I could focus on was the action in the basement.

The glorious action.

As The Bully became conscious he found himself exactly where I placed him: sitting at The Battle Station in front of his own monitor. The Subject sat across from him at his laptop.

Ready for war.

The Bully was still chained and locked in position. He wasn't able to stand from his seat, or even move his chair that much, but I did loosen the grip a bit. This provided him with just enough freedom to shift his arms and hands.

This freedom was vital. I needed liberated limbs so The Bully could type and attack his opponent, thus showing me if The Subject had any trace of tough skin.

That was the point of this test.

But it was becoming increasingly clear that my plans were destined for redirection.

I figured all of The Bully's moaning and sobbing would drain away by the time I positioned him at The Battle Station. I figured this arrangement would provide him with a feeling of comfort. And once he was in his comfort zone, I truly felt The Bully's dominant mentality would take effect.

It did not.

No matter how often I explained the purpose of Test #3, no matter how many times I shouted downstairs and demanded him to begin, The Bully just whined about how badly he wanted to see his family.

I shouted down at The Bully that if he didn't torment The Subject he would never again see his loved ones. More crying ensued after that statement. It was becoming outrageous.

During this exchange, The Subject sat calmly behind his laptop, smirking devilishly at The Bully and occasionally drooling. When The Bully's tears lessened, the basement became so quiet I could hear large drops of spittle leave The Subject's mouth and splash onto his keyboard.

The Subject was the insatiable one. The Bully had become nothing more than a sniveling jellyfish. This did not fit my initial design.

But I was willing to let the situation move forward.

I just needed to give the proper push.

I did so by entering the basement and placing a butcher knife to The Bully's throat. He promised to cooperate after that threat. I then returned to my monitors.

I had one camera zoomed in closely on The Bully's screen. This way I could see his text clearly, as well as The Subject's responses.

The Bully's first message to The Subject read: "Can you help me? Please!"

The Subject stared expressionlessly at the message before finally typing his response: "No."

The Bully: "Why not? Please! I'm not supposed to be here!"

No response from The Subject.

The Bully: "Where am I? Can you please tell me that? I just want to go home! I want to see my parents!"

No response from The Subject.

This lack of reaction enraged The Bully. His breathing became heavier and his right foot jumped up and down in agitation. Much like The Subject's foot during his date. Right before he raped Pepper. This was good.

The Bully: "You need to help me out. That crazy fucker put a knife to my throat! You need to help me before he does something worse!"

The Subject offered nothing but a widening grin.

The Bully: "If you don't help me out…"

Pause. Pause. Pause.

The Bully: "I swear…"

Once The Bully's "I swear" appeared on both screens The Subject hungrily moved to his keyboard and wrote: "You swear wut?"

The Bully emitted three firm breaths before typing: "I swear, I'll kick your ass."

Far from the most intimidating message.

The Subject's first chuckle was disturbing. I had never heard him make that type of noise. I had never heard *anyone* make that type of noise. Although it was a chuckle, it contained so much animated bitterness that it sounded more like a vehicle backfiring upon ignition.

I found it alarming from where I sat. From all the way upstairs. Imagine how The Bully felt sitting so close.

It only became worse when The Subject's chuckle grew more extreme and metamorphosed into maniacal cackling. This was him calling The Bully's bluff. Calling it by laughing in his face and then slamming his fists onto the desk, shaking not only The Battle Station but also The Bully's will to retaliate.

Then came The Subject's typing. Spirited and full of fire. It was some of the vilest words I've ever read. And it was done in such a speedy manner. I don't believe The Subject even had to think before typing. The nastiness was already inside of him. Automatic.

"Ur gonna kick my ass?" The Subject wrote. "Go ahead, u fruit. Stick your foot up my ass. I'll snap it off while it's up there. I'll rip it right off ur leg and shove it down ur throat. U hear me, faggot? I'll make u eat my shit and choke on it."

The Bully's eyes widened as the wickedness amplified. He tried to keep his chin raised. He tried to stay strong. But it was easy to see his lower lip quiver.

"Wat?" The Subject continued. "U got nothing to say? U think silence will work against me? How bout I use my daddy's knife to cut out your tongue? Then u b really silent."

That was a very revealing message.

The Subject referred to me as his "daddy." Never once had I told him he was my offspring.

I suppose at some point throughout the experiment he had developed that image of me.

I wasn't freaked out. I wasn't upset for getting too close. I was somewhat proud.

Not so much about the actual designation. More about my ability to have such an influence over another. It was quite an accomplishment.

The other revealing aspect involved The Subject's astuteness. Even though he was focused on his computer as I held the knife to The Bully's throat he still mentally stored the threat for when he needed it.

"Yeh, that's rite." The Subject proceeded, realizing he hit a nerve. "After I cut out ur tongue I'll slice that ugly ass face of urs. I already have problems looking at it. It won't make much of a difference. HA HA HA!"

The Subject actually wrote out the *Ha's*.

"And while I'm at it, I'll cut off ur dick to. And ur balls. I'll stick ur dick in ur ass cuz ur a fag and I'll send ur balls to ur parents for making such a stupid kid."

The reference to The Bully's parents was like detonating an emotional bomb. It was as if The Subject reminded his opponent of how far away he was from love and safety, all the while hinting that he might never again see his parents.

It was too much for The Bully to handle.

He wept immensely and plead with The Subject. He didn't use the keyboard in front of him. He vocalized his begging. He told The Subject he would do whatever necessary to be liberated.

Contrary to The Bully's actions, The Subject didn't articulate his response. He typed his message. He typed calmly and with great poise.

"Kill yourself."

The Subject nodded at the pistol in the basement as soon as he typed his message.

He nodded and smirked.

This nod showed The Bully that he had only one way of escaping the basement. That his only road to freedom involved putting a bullet in his own head.

This was The Subject's point of view.

It wasn't entirely incorrect. But there were in fact other options. Two more, to be exact.

I could've gone down to the basement and released The Bully. *Technically*, that was an option.

If I did take that route, I would have had to make sure I wasn't sloppy.

If The Bully was released without alteration, he would've ran off to the nearest police station, threatening my own independence. I couldn't have that. So if I were to free The Bully I would've first had to perform neurological modification. I would've had to make sure his memory became undependable. Perhaps I would've given him one concussion per week, for many weeks, until he lost his ability to recall information.

But no. This would not happen. I couldn't let it happen. It would've taken too much time out of my schedule.

So that option was scratched.

The Bully's other option was for him to grab the gun and end The Subject's life. Although I would've been upset by that decision, I still would've accepted the outcome.

I would've let The Bully kill The Subject.

In fact, that is exactly what he attempted to do.

Attempted.

***

I know The Bully *wanted* to kill The Subject. Whether or not he would've ultimately pulled the trigger, that's difficult to call. He never actually made it to that point.

After The Subject wrote for his opponent to commit suicide, The Bully responded by shouting, "Kill *myself*?! No! Fuck you!"

But The Bully's *you* was cut short.

As he was ending his statement he reached for the pistol, to probably murder The Subject, and as he grabbed the weapon he was shocked by 50,000 volts of electricity, all thanks to my homemade device.

The Bully immediately withdrew and, wanting to cool the sting, tried bringing his hand to his mouth. But his movement was restricted by the chains.

The Bully screamed at the ceiling of the basement and pleaded for some mystery savior to unlock his shackles. He screamed that he couldn't spend another second "trapped" next to a "psychopath." He then looked down and realized he urinated in his pants.

His crying started up once again.

The kid sure did cry a lot.

I turned to tell #1 to clean The Bully, but my colleague was no longer on the couch. I figured he was off scrubbing another room.

Refusing to do any cleaning myself, I left The Bully to soak in his own piss. It was only urine. It was bound to dry at some point.

Although it was only urine, it did provide The Subject with ammunition.

He wrote to The Bully: "It stinks in here. How much piss dropped outta ur pussy?"

The Bully didn't respond.

The Subject continued: "U must wanna die. I know if I was a stupid piece of shit like u I wud wanna die. There's honestly no reason for u to live. U will never beat me. U will never get outta here. Ur to stupid. U are the dumbest and ugliest faggot I have ever seen. You can't last down here. One way or another you will die in that seat. It might be 60 years from now. It might be by my hands. U will die in this basement."

More weeping from The Bully.

I remember wondering about what was more traumatic for him to visualize. Dying naturally as a prisoner in the basement? Or being murdered by The Subject?

Personally? I had an issue with the former. I didn't have another sixty years on this planet. So I was hoping things would conclude at a faster pace.

Fortunately, the human mind isn't excellent when it comes to patience.

Results arrived two weeks after the urinated pants incident. Once The Bully finally lost *his* patience.

In the grand scheme of things, two weeks is not a long period. For me and my research, the two weeks were actually agreeable and enlightening. For The Subject, for the most part, the two weeks were a blast since he was able to do exactly what he wanted. For The Bully, the two weeks leading up to the final result were horrendous.

Absolute agony.

First came the mental torture, which had actually been going on for a while, particularly in relation to the sixty year message. But The Subject didn't ease up after that. His messages remained on that same level of callousness.

He repeatedly wrote spiteful comments regarding The Bully's appearance and his sexuality. He told The Bully that no one loved him. Especially not his parents. He drove this point deeper by telling The Bully that his parents wouldn't miss him after his death.

The Bully didn't hold up well against this barrage. He carried on with the crying and prayed to see his mother. And, showing that his fight had all but vanished, he never again reached for the pistol.

It's funny. He could have easily grabbed the weapon without any issues at that point in the test. I had deliberately turned off the electricity from upstairs using my remote control. No shock would've occurred.

But The Bully never made another attempt.

He just cried a lot.

Looking back now, The Bully's crying might've had more to do with him being abducted and locked in a basement and force-fed and unwillingly injected with various drugs to make him sleep and then make him wake up, and less to do with being insulted on a two-person message board.

It's tough to know for sure though.

What I do know is that, on Day 14, everything amplified when the mental torture shifted into the lane of the physical.

NOTE #13

KAREN: *Did this young man ever try to talk you out of force-feeding him?*

DR. RAVENSDALE: *Most of the time he just choked on what I made him ingest. He also cried due to being so alarmed. But there was one instance where he did ask me quite the simple question. He didn't ask me to let him go. He didn't ask for help. He just asked, "Why are you doing this to me?"*

KAREN: *What did you say?*

DR. RAVENSDALE: *I said, "You did this to yourself, Johnny." After that he just kept pleading with me and telling me over and over that he was a good kid. "I'm a good kid. I'm a good kid. I'm a good kid. I'm a good kid."*

KAREN: *Wait, if I remember correctly, his name wasn't Johnny.*

DR. RAVENSDALE: *The Bully's? No. That wasn't his name. Why?*

KAREN: *Who is Johnny?*

DR. RAVENSDALE: *Johnny? Why do you want...*

KAREN: *You said the name Johnny.*

DR. RAVENSDALE: *I did? Well, I don't want to talk about that. I was twelve years old anyway. It doesn't matter now.*

KAREN: *But I think...*

DR. RAVENSDALE: *Enough!*

The Subject was determinedly typing abusive messages when The Bully finally snapped. He slammed his fist on The Battle Station and shouted, "Stop it! STOP IT RIGHT NOW!"

The basement was unnervingly silent for a moment.

Then The Bully continued, "You're not hurting me. There's nothing you can do to hurt me!"

The Subject didn't smile or scowl. He didn't grunt. He didn't touch his keyboard. He didn't do anything for a full minute but watch The Bully. It wasn't an angry stare. Nor was it one exhibiting exhilaration. It was simply a blank stare.

As soon as minute two began, The Subject stood from his chair like an unflustered warrior and advanced toward The Bully. The more The Subject moved, the more The Bully tried to shrink and disappear.

With his feet now firmly planted, his hands linked behind his back, The Subject stood stone-faced over his opponent until The Bully broke the silence and whispered, "You don't want this. You don't want to hurt me."

It was said in a tone of desperation.

The Subject slowly opened his mouth, the widening process reminding me of a bubble expanding in size, and emitted strange guttural sounds. Like a confounded and irate ape. It was as if he wanted to speak but couldn't find the right way to articulate his ideas.

Following his sixth animal-like wheeze, The Subject hastily turned around and grabbed the pistol from the small end table. He was making a big move.

I was glad I had remembered to turn off the electricity on the pistol. I had a feeling that by doing so I'd be keeping things interesting.

I was right.

The Bully winced a great deal. He tried his best to wriggle free from his chains, but all he could to do was push his chair a few inches from The Battle Station. The sounds of the wheel-less chair scraping against the basement floor hurt my eardrums.

The movement of the chair also exposed The Bully's bare feet.

The Subject saw this and fired a bullet into his opponent's right foot.

The howls of agony were beyond thunderous. Way louder than the scraping of the chair's legs. So loud that I had to remove my headphones and use the speakers.

Thanks to this experiment, I had seen some unbelievable and vehement deeds. But, until that moment, I had never seen anything like that shooting. Not in my entire career.

Even at the hospital, I had seen some truly terrible injuries and lacerations. Irreparable damages. Patients becoming paralyzed. You name it. But I had never seen such sudden and explosive violence.

The way The Bully's foot erupted was shocking and extraordinary. It looked like someone arranged a row of bananas and smashed them with a steel beam.

If The Bully somehow didn't think he was doomed before that shot was fired, he certainly did now.

***

The Bully's foot would never heal. Especially since I did nothing to treat it.

As time went on, the appendage formed into nothing more than a useless and pulverized piece of chaos, becoming incredibly black and gangrenous.

Things weren't looking good for the former high school star.

When the pain started to slightly diminish, allowing the wounded one to form a coherent sentence, The Bully made it clear that he was accepting his situation.

Five days after the shooting, following one hundred and twenty hours of asinine mumbling and slobbering on himself, The Bully finally cried, "I don't want to die. I don't want to die."

He repeated this statement over and over.

This showed his awareness. Showed that he understood the real possibility of his death.

The Subject took advantage of his opponent's feebleness. He turned his laptop to face The Bully and showed him videos of people being tortured and executed. Whenever The Bully tried to close his eyes and escape the footage, The Subject slapped him hard across the face. If the slap didn't work, The Subject stood behind The Bully holding open his eyelids. A technique he learned from me.

The Subject made sure The Bully watched countless videos exhibiting cruelty and slaughters. It was like a brand new way of cyberbullying.

Following three days of being force-fed nonstop torture porn, with his foot beyond infected and in need of amputation, The Bully finally surrendered and weakly sobbed, "I can't...I can't take it anymore."

At this statement, The Subject paused his current video — a snuff film where one guy anally raped a thirteen year-old girl while another guy removed her teeth with corroded pliers — and hungrily stared into his victim's eyes.

He knew exactly what The Bully said.

But he wanted more.

He snorted at The Bully as if to say: "Go on, you can say it."

The Bully responded by unsteadily uttering, "Just do it. If you're going to kill me, just do it already."

He then shed a few more puny tears.

The Bully was too shattered and exhausted for any grand spectacle, yet too close to death not to weep.

The Subject moved his laptop back to The Battle Station and removed the pistol from the waist of his filthy jeans.

The pistol was aimed and a flash emerged.

Though not from the weapon.

Not yet.

The flash developed within The Bully's eyes as he realized his finale was approaching. There was an odd yet excellent serenity that washed over his face. He was making peace with his end.

Then The Subject fired four shots.

Two bullets penetrated The Bully's thighs. The other two soared through his shoulders. None of the four bullets killed him.

This is exactly what The Subject wanted. More suffering.

The Bully spent the next two days nearly bleeding to death. It was excruciating to hear. I couldn't imagine how excruciating it must've *felt*.

I did administer a small amount of morphine to help with the pain. But not too much. I didn't want to interfere with the experiment.

I also did not surgically remove the two bullets from his thighs. Nor did I stitch him to stop the unceasing flow of body fluid.

The Subject did nothing either to relieve The Bully's pain. I didn't anticipate him helping, but I didn't expect him to make matters worse for his opponent, which he did.

The Subject took his laptop from The Battle Station and held it with one hand in front of The Bully's sallow face. With his free hand, The Subject alternated between typing indecent messages and playing more videos of people being slayed.

Some say that when an individual is sick or injured that a positive mindset can help their health. As a Doctor, I've always felt it's best to stick with actual medication. But I will admit that a positive mindset does not hurt. On the opposite end of the spectrum, a negative mindset while sick or injured is far from advantageous.

Those videos of people being impaled, shot, burned and tortured, as well as being berated on a message board, did not provide any aid to The Bully's deteriorating brain.

The anguish and mental punishment left The Bully even more defeated. His screams had long become whimpers. His tears had gone from a steady flow to nothing more than occasional drips. Similar to a leaking faucet.

He had nothing left.

The Bully clumsily reached toward The Subject's laptop and used the keyboard to write a message. Although the message was only two words, it took him a long time to type it out.

Do it.

That was it. A simple statement.

All he wanted now was death.

The Subject was happy to oblige.

In his own way.

The Subject stood over The Bully. In one hand remained his laptop. In the other was the pistol. He wasn't necessarily aiming the weapon at The Bully. But he wasn't pointing it away from him either.

The Subject placed the pistol in The Bully's hand. A maneuver that triggered my uneasiness. The Bully used every ounce of energy he had to raise the weapon, aiming it at The Subject's chest. My heart was pounding. But The Subject remained calm. He didn't flinch at all. He stared down the barrel of the pistol. The weapon I purchased.

As my heart rate continued to escalate, so did The Bully's trembling. Moisture formed on his forehead as he tried to pull the trigger. He was giving it all he had. And then, just as he built up enough energy to kill The Subject, he discovered that his effort was useless.

Unbeknownst to both me and The Bully, The Subject had flipped the pistol's safety switch, leaving his foe to struggle without result and use his very last drop of energy.

The Subject laughed like a hyperactive hyena and The Bully dropped his arm into his lap. The gun was still in his hand. But he was too weak to try again.

The Subject smiled and grabbed his laptop. He leaned close to The Bully while searching online for: Happy Family — Mother, father, son.

The Subject clicked on the first picture that appeared. The family members in the photo were enjoying a lovely afternoon in the park. They were all smiling. Bountifully elated.

As soon as The Bully saw the image he had a Simple Partial Seizure. The photo definitely triggered memories of his own family. The one he would never see again.

Once the muscle contractions were over, The Subject took hold of The Bully's hand, the hand still holding the weapon, and brought it up to his rival's head. He turned off the pistol's safety. The Bully's finger was still on the trigger. The Subject wrapped his finger around The Bully's.

It all happened very fast.

The Bully said the words, "Mom...I."

Cutting him off, The Subject pulled The Bully's finger which in turn pulled the trigger, putting a bullet in his own head.

The Bully was lifeless.

Mom...I.

Mom...I.

The Bully's last words.

The Bully's blood oozed onto the basement floor, slithering around the bits of skull and chunks of intelligence. The Subject gave a simple nod and moved back to The Battle Station with his laptop.

He was the victor. He had bullied The Bully to death.

With his job complete, he continued watching videos of assaults and murders.

It was his time to relax.

Not mine.

I had to sterilize the basement. A large job considering that #1 no longer helped with that type of dirty work. Even if I asked, my former colleague would've provided some lame excuse about cleaning the rest of the laboratory.

What a piece of garbage!

I really wanted to hurt him.

But I knew I had to concentrate on more important matters.

Before I began washing the basement, I filled a syringe with a large dose of Butorphanol. The Subject seemed quite comfortable in front of his laptop, but I still didn't want to risk anything. He had been active for so long, and pumped with so much Pentedrone throughout the test, that I feared he might snap while I was in his vicinity.

I couldn't have that happen, so I had to put him out.

He didn't struggle as I searched for a vein and inserted the needle.

I didn't even bother bringing him to his bed once the injection was complete. I just let him fall asleep at The Battle Station.

The cleaning took a day and a half.

Along with the scrubbing, I also had to dig the hole myself. I used the spot where #2 and Pepper were already buried. The soil was softer there. But the process still knocked me out.

Once the hole was dug, I dragged The Bully upstairs and out to the backyard. I bagged him first so blood didn't leak over the laboratory. But even the solid grip provided by the tarp wasn't much help.

Halfway up the basement steps, while my fatigue and aching back made me unsure about advancement, I started imagining scenarios that could've possibly helped my situation. I thought about dropping The Bully back down to the basement where I could acidify his body. I then thought about hacking his corpse so I'd be able to move pieces instead of one large section. I also thought that, with the proper videos, I could possibly teach The Subject about cannibalism and provide him with a feast.

But I thought better of these ideas. They would've been overly time-consuming.

I knew if I just pushed myself through the pain I'd be able to finish the task.

Once the body and all other materials were buried, except for the pistol, I began scrubbing the basement as thoroughly as possible. Some of the blood was easy to sop up. Some had coagulated, which helped. But a good amount had fused with the basement floor.

With that there was only so much I could do.

The odor of the carnage mixed with the cleaning agents was strong. So potent that I became a bit lightheaded.

Considering the possible pollutants floating around the atmosphere, I thought about removing The Subject from the basement. I then thought otherwise when I felt the exhaustion hijack my body.

I injected The Subject with another large dose of Butorphanol and went upstairs to catch a few hours of rest, figuring my experiment would continue without issue when I awoke.

I had no clue that everything was about to change.

Test #4 - Sweating It Out

I gathered as much equipment as I could. I did so as fast as possible. I needed to. I had no other choice but to act quickly.

I collected some audio and video equipment. Clothing. Some food. I looked for The Subject's tracker, but was unable to locate the device. This worried me. I didn't want him getting lost.

I woke The Subject and got him moving.

I rented a motel room relatively far away from my laboratory.

As for #1, as it's now known, that bastard was the reason I fled so rapidly.

A few days following the conclusion of Test #3, I woke up to a completely spotless laboratory. My first thought was: *Finally*!

It felt like #1 took forever to sterilize the place.

My second reaction involved uneasiness.

This anxiety commenced when I spotted the used bottle of Arsenic and the syringe I used to kill #2. They were both on the kitchen table. Next to those items was a note written by #1. It was short, surprisingly clear and articulate.

The note read: *I know what you've done.*

Shit!

I loathe re-experiencing this period because it reminds me of the guilt I felt. The unnecessary guilt, I should say.

As soon as I saw the empty bottle my stomach jumped and my brain said, "Oh no!"

I did quickly shake that mindset. But I'm still upset with it being my initial reaction. As if I had something to feel guilty about!

What I did was right!

If I was in the same exact situation today with the same exact opportunity, I would terminate #2 in the same exact fashion.

He presented danger. He lacked devotion. He possessed an obvious aversion for the way I handled my experiment. This was all grounds for dismissal.

If I hadn't murdered that fucking pillock, there's no telling what #2 would've done once he healed.

Sure, worst case scenario, he would've done exactly what #1 wound up doing. But he would've done so a lot sooner. This would've stopped me from obtaining the great results of Test #3.

And Test #4 for that matter.

Prior to fleeing, after reading his note and understanding the bedlam he was bound to create, I sprinted around the laboratory searching for #1. I had to make the effort, although I knew it was useless. I knew he was gone.

What I didn't know was how long it had been since he left. Nor did I know if he went directly to the police or somewhere else to relax. I couldn't be certain.

Not knowing how much time I had on my side, I had no other choice but to move swiftly and keep an eye out for a squad car pulling up in my drive.

I stuffed all the materials into my rental car and then injected The Subject. I needed him sleeping and easy to transport.

I grabbed the pistol and felt a curious uncertainty wash over me. I didn't know why I grabbed the weapon. I still don't. I don't think I would've opened fire if the police arrived at my laboratory. All I know is it felt good to have the weapon on my person. I felt protected.

With the essentials packed in my rental car, I gave the laboratory one last look and sped off, all the while dwelling on the evidence I was leaving in the dust.

As I now sit in this padded cell, I am very aware of *everything* I left behind, especially since the prosecutor provided the details during my case.

What a bunch of snakes and vultures!

The journalists wrote that I left too much evidence to ever be considered a criminal mastermind. What a joke!

First of all, you harebrained cunts, it was never my goal to be a criminal mastermind. I am a man of academic exploration! A man of experimental discovery!

"He's not a criminal mastermind," wrote those shitbags.

Fuck them!

They will never understand the amount of pressure I felt bolting from that laboratory. They will never understand how badly I tried to keep my experiment alive. Like they could ever comprehend anything as momentous as my life's work. They could never and will never appreciate such brilliance.

So what do they do?

They take the route of lackadaisicalness and criticize me blindly.

Allow me to repeat…Fuck them!

***

The Motel was a good distance away from the laboratory. I arrived relatively late. 10:53pm.

That's what the clock read in my rental car. I left my watch at the house, so I couldn't be totally certain.

I could've arrived sooner but, not wanting anyone to see me transport my materials, I drove around until I felt the time was right.

The desk clerk wasn't interested in anything but collecting my money. When I asked for a room in the back she merely grunted and handed me the keys. Room 437. I paid for a week's worth of stay. I wasn't sure if I'd need that much time. All I knew is that I didn't want to be bothered.

I used The Bully's Grandmother's wheelchair to transport The Subject into the motel room and directly into the bathroom. I hoisted his body into the bathtub and positioned him as straight as possible. I grabbed a pillow from the bed and placed it behind The Subject's neck.

I mention the pillow to show that I am not the man the news has made me out to be. I am not a complete monster. Would a monster want The Subject to wake up comfortably? I don't believe so.

When I finished inserting the pillow behind The Subject, I set up various cameras around the bathroom. With Test #4, I knew The Subject would come unglued and possibly break one of my cameras. I didn't care about damaged equipment in terms of money. I cared about fully capturing the results. So the more the better.

Once the cameras were arranged, I prepared the rest of the equipment from my old laboratory. Not much. Just a small monitor and a speaker.

I then closed the bathroom door, dragged over the small motel couch, flipped the piece of furniture and propped it in front of the bathroom door.

For safe measure, I also moved the room's stained loveseat and jammed it between the couch and the wall directly outside the bathroom.

Since the bathroom door opened into the motel room The Subject would not be able to escape unless I let him out myself.

If you've read all the articles about me and this particular test, if you believed such defamation, you might consider me to be some sort of "Psychopath". That's the word used by the journalists. But they couldn't have been more mistaken about my character. Surprise surprise.

The real reason I systematically locked The Subject inside that bathroom is because, no matter how desperate he eventually became, I couldn't have him finding a way out of this test. I couldn't have him sullying my results.

I knew The Subject would become frantic with the agony he would soon feel. If I didn't block the exit he would've battered down the door and ruined my work.

That's why I did what I did.

That occupational mindset was my constant influence.

Do you finally understand?

Every maneuver I pulled was for my experiment. *Everything* I've ever done has been linked with understanding the human psyche, particularly in relation to the technological age.

That's why I conducted in that motel room what would be my last test.

Not because I wanted to "abandon" my experiment like a "Psychopath." No. Because I wanted to see if The Subject could stay away from technology for a stretch while also becoming a functioning member of society.

This was the whole point of Test #4.

I needed to isolate The Subject. Remove him from the only world he understood. Strip him of his comforts. And with that, I hoped that he would break away from the world he knew and find the path to becoming a brand new individual.

NOTE #14

KAREN: *You must've known this plan was bound to fail.*

DR. RAVENSDALE: Nothing I've ever done has failed. Correct yourself.

KAREN: Sorry. But you must've known this would not end well.

DR. RAVENSDALE: You must be referring to what happened after the test, because the results of this test were brilliant.

KAREN: According to your former colleague…

DR. RAVENSDALE: Which one?

KAREN: Which one? The one who is still alive. #1.

DR. RAVENSDALE: Oh…Well…What did that little shit say?

KAREN: He said the results of Test #4 show that you don't actually care about scientific discovery. He said the results show that you only care about creating mayhem.

DR. RAVENSDALE: Creating mayhem? That's what he said? What else? Tell me right now!

KAREN: I don't want to upset you.

DR. RAVENSDALE: Say it!

KAREN: He said you only care about torturing the innocent and destroying humanity and that he is ashamed to have ever been so influenced and manipulated by you. And there are many who believe him. There are many who believe that he's currently on suicide watch because of this whole experiment.

DR. RAVENSDALE: The only thing destroying humanity is spineless pieces of garbage like #1. That pathetic cunt. I wish the guards on his suicide watch would take a night off.

The Subject had to sweat it out. He needed to axe his addiction to technology.

I left him in the bathroom with a few bars of packaged food and the pillow.

I genuinely believed that would be enough.

Once The Subject awoke it took him some time to accept his situation. With all the medication in his system it was difficult for him to defeat disequilibrium. I had injected him so often for so many years that I was somewhat astonished about the functionality of his organs.

When his brain grasped what his eyes observed, The Subject felt a strong aversion for his environment. His confusion emerged at first. With a croaky groan and some cracking bones, The Subject crawled out of the bathtub, glancing around suspiciously at his surroundings the entire time.

He made a move for the door.

He turned the knob and pushed. This effort was of course unsuccessful.

He turned around and saw himself in the mirror. This was the first time The Subject saw his own image. I suppose at some point he might have caught his reflection in one of his monitors, but the odds on that were low. He was always too invested in his research. So I was fairly convinced that, for the first time in his eighteen-year life, The Subject was finally seeing his face.

It wasn't a handsome face. Nor was it a hideous one. His features were certainly weathered, especially for someone his age, but this wasn't surprising. It was expected considering his intake of medication and his almost complete lack of exposure to the outside world.

But none of this seemed to matter anyway.

The Subject didn't care whether he was attractive or ugly. He was simply amazed and startled that he was actually putting a face to himself.

A face to his thoughts.

A face to his activities and all he exemplified.

The Subject approached the mirror timidly, but also with a sense that he *had to* inspect. Like a veterinarian stumbling upon an aggrieved yet mephitic snake.

The more he advanced the more his hand raised toward his reflection. Upon reaching his target, The Subject placed his hand on the mirror and used his thumb to rub the reflection of his cheek. His whole body shook as his massaging increased in force. Then, quite unexpectedly, The Subject exploded and cried tears so enormous they could've drowned a human soul.

He cried and cried and cried. He did his best to avoid his own reflection, but he almost always immediately looked back to stare once again.

This would bring about more sobbing.

After a while of this behavior, the frustration kicked in.

The Subject spun away from the mirror and rushed toward the bathroom door, repeatedly using his shoulder like a battering ram in attempt to gain freedom. But again, The Subject's exertion was ineffective.

I had done an excellent job with his confinement.

Unable to breakout, The Subject turned around, charged at the mirror, and destroyed the reflecting surface to bits.

The more The Subject punched the more the mirror shattered. The more the mirror shattered the more The Subject's flesh opened. An eruption of gore.

Blood sprayed everywhere.

A great deal stained the bathroom walls. Some drenched the shards of broken mirror. The rest collected in the sink below The Subject, especially since he inadvertently closed the drain during his outburst.

Still leaking, The Subject reached down and grabbed a broken piece of mirror. He wanted to inspect himself. This particular piece was heavily soaked in blood. The Subject couldn't get the best look, but it was still clear enough to exhibit his features.

Refusing his appearance, The Subject dropped the glass into the toilet and flushed it down. He turned back to the sink where he cupped a tiny pool of blood in his palms and dragged his hands over his face, turning his cheeks crimson.

He looked like a soldier. A nefarious warrior *very* prepared to murder.

I was quite glad to have him locked in that bathroom.

With his face covered in blood, The Subject made his way back to the bathtub and crawled inside. He closed his eyes and tried to fall asleep.

This wasn't happening. Rest would not appear.

The Subject writhed and wrestled with himself until his eyes bolted open and he began shouting. But it wasn't his normal brand of racket. It wasn't his gravelly groans and screeches. The Subject actually shouted coherent statements.

"Where am I?!" The Subject yelled. "Help me! Where the fuck am I?"

The Subject got out of the tub and slammed his fist into the bathroom door, cracking the inexpensive wood.

"Get me out of here! I need my home, you bastard! I need my home!"

I never considered the basement to be much of a home. I never wanted it to be. All I desired was for it to represent a place of business. But I suppose one can only understand what they observe.

I suppose if someone exists in nothing but a hole they're bound to consider that hole their home.

"Dad!? Dad!? Are you there?" The Subject continued, referring to me. "I can't be here! I need my computer! Please!!!"

He was hooked.

I pondered whether a response would be counterproductive. I didn't believe The Subject knew I was directly on the other side of the door. Part of me didn't want to ruin that uncertainty.

On the other hand, I also felt the sooner The Subject knew he'd be without technology the sooner he'd be able to recover.

So I moved toward the bathroom door, or as close to it as possible, and shouted, "That will not happen, son. You will not return home anytime soon. You will not be using your computer."

The Subject flipped. His screams returned to his customary beastliness and he began thrashing the bathroom. He punched the cheap walls, breaking some tiles and a couple of not-so-cheap cameras.

The scene had become hectic.

I powered on the room's television and raised the volume to drown out the pandemonium. Just in case.

The motel was fairly unoccupied. And the caliber of people *actually* renting rooms weren't ones to stick their noses into the business of others. But there's nothing wrong with a little carefulness.

I think it was a wise move.

Just as I raised the volume, The Subject clutched the sink and ripped the device from the wall. It only took him three attempts.

Water blasted everywhere, soaking the bathroom, collecting in puddles on the floor, saturating The Subject. This caused further invigoration.

The Subject dropped to his knees in front of the exposed pipes and let the water wash the remaining blood from his face. He feverishly laughed as this took place, occasionally choking on the liquid firing down his throat.

His laughter sounded homicidal.

This turned out to be appropriate, given what he shouted next.

When his clothes became overly waterlogged, The Subject exposed his inflamed skin by ripping the garments off his body and shouting, "I am going to kill you! Kill YOU! KILL YOU! I am going to kill you!"

He screamed this repeatedly. It got to the point where his threat almost sounded harmonious. Like the refrain to a disturbed song.

I did not enjoy this.

I felt as if I had been backstabbed.

How dare The Subject say a thing like that! To *me*! He was nothing more than my seed of experimentation. My test dummy. *I* was the one doing the work. *I* was the one making the breakthroughs. And off he went chanting about murdering me. I viewed this as intolerable interference. As him wanting to sabotage my test.

I already had to contend with my colleagues' betrayal. It pained me to think that I had to deal with it once more with my own Subject.

It was unacceptable.

I let the test continue. But, at that point, I was displeased with the results.

The Subject's bad attitude didn't subside. He actually became worse. More psychotic. His body twitched severely and he continually yelled the word: "Screen!"

He then grabbed a shard of glass from the sodden floor and punctured his chest. The blood surged from his wound like a mudflow.

Bright.

Red.

Thick.

The Subject dipped two fingers into his laceration and used the blood to draw a childlike rectangle on the bathroom wall. I realized almost instantly that he was drawing a computer monitor.

The Subject drew another rectangle beneath the drawing of the monitor, this one with several tiny squares within.

A keyboard.

The Subject stepped back to admire his work. He then attacked like a man possessed, poking the drawing as if he wanted to find the end of the internet.

This of course was impossible.

Realizing the pointlessness of his actions, The Subject stopped typing and let his blood slide down the wall in slim, gooey streams.

Watching his own hope evaporate was too much for The Subject to handle.

Incensed, he slammed his forehead three times against the tiled wall. On the second go, another tile dislodged from its position. On the third and hardest headbutt, The Subject went unconscious.

The Subject fell rearward and smashed the back of his cranium against the tub, once again opening himself up. The tub was no longer completely white.

There was so much blood in that bathroom. So much that it looked like an operation gone terribly wrong.

I was convinced The Subject was a goner. The type of impact he suffered made me believe the experiment had come to an end…

…But not quite.

The Subject awoke approximately two hours later, screaming the high-pitched shouts of man unable to escape a nightmare.

This was the first time he exhibited real panic. Prior to that moment, his shouting was always more aggressive and confrontational.

Not anymore.

He was in terrible pain. In dire need of medical attention. I initially believed that his anguish was linked with neurological trauma from the fall. But I started understanding the truth when The Subject couldn't stop shaking long enough to get off floor.

I had seen this behavior a number of times during my years at the hospital. I knew the deal as soon as I heard The Subject's teeth chattering and witnessed his inability to possess warmth. He was experiencing more than one version of withdrawal.

In my rushed departure I forgot to grab the medication from my laboratory.

Was this a horrible mistake?

I'd have to say no.

Even if I brought the medication, I'm not sure I would've injected The Subject. He was an incarcerated monster. Unquestionably fragile at that point, but a monster nonetheless. And if there is one certainty in life, besides death, it's that one must never get too close to an incarcerated monster.

I was also still upset about his murderous chant.

How dare he?

He wanted to kill me, kill me, kill me.

Then he wanted my assistance?

The Subject waved farewell to that as soon as he mentioned his homicidal intent. That little traitor.

***

The following day was beyond unpleasant. For The Subject, that is. His drug withdrawal had completely taken over. There were times when he couldn't stop his shakes and cold sweats. Other times he tried tearing off his burning skin. There were also moments where he'd claw at bathroom floor, almost as if this scraping could lead to his freedom.

The heaving began not long after that. Fierce bouts of vomiting that brought static to my speakers and vibrations to the motel room. It was quite the potent battle. I felt like I could taste his suffering.

The Subject was in a dangerous zone.

I understood the seriousness when he began weeping, not from frustration, but from the feeling that death was around the corner.

I had never seen The Subject reveal such vulnerability. It was disgusting. I was embarrassed for him. Embarrassed about his weakness. He was once such a strong individual. Now he was vomiting and quivering on the floor of a motel bathroom.

Yes, like some of the others throughout my experiment, I realized that it was me who put him in that position. But far more important than that, while watching his embarrassing display of weakness, I also realized the high possibility of The Subject not surviving Test #4.

His symptoms were too dire. His surroundings too wretched and unaccommodating. Knowing this made me want to put an end to the test. It made me want to move the furniture and open the bathroom door. Odds are it would've been safe to do so. The Subject was far too delicate to snap into an attack mode.

But I couldn't do it.

I could not let him go free.

There are several reasons why.

Firstly, I've never allowed any interference with my experiment. Why would I start then? Secondly, as The Subject displayed misery that I had only seen in my worst patients, while defecating and ejecting sickness all over the floor, although the toilet was no more than two feet away, I realized that the test had altered. It was no longer about The Subject conquering his addiction to technology. It grew it something much larger.

The test became: Can The Subject defeat *me*.

Throughout every test in my experiment, even if it wasn't the plan, The Subject developed a rivalry with another. It was usually with someone who got in the way of his cravings.

I understood this.

Hell, I've personally felt the importance of competition.

I developed rivalries with two people that started out as my colleagues. I clearly bested #2. And although #1 helped put me in this cell, I still believe I will eventually be considered the victor.

#1 will be seen as the man who turned his back on this great experiment. I'll be seen as the impressive mind who changed the world.

All of this leads to me having no problems with rivalries.

What I do have a problem with is losing, which is why I did not let The Subject exit that bathroom.

***

Watching The Subject wither away was something else. I wouldn't say it was pleasurable. Nor would was it unsettling.

It was enlightening.

The more The Subject agonized the more I realized I no longer needed him. I had already discovered so much. I had been observing him for nearly twenty years. That's a solid record.

Could I have learned more if I cleared the furniture and helped him survive? Of course.

The question is: Did I want to?

There are two answers to that.

1) I never want to stop learning. So a small part of me says yes.

2) On the other hand, the larger part of me says no since adjustments in life must be made. My own adjustment involved me no longer wanting to learn from The Subject.

Being threatened by him really pissed me off. I simply didn't like him anymore.

Who the hell did that piece of shit think he was?

I didn't care if he couldn't see straight and just lashed out. I couldn't accept that. I created that ungrateful mongrel. I was his master. And if I felt like letting him die then so be it. Nothing would stop me. Particularly not sympathy.

And that death is exactly what happened.

The Subject could no longer handle the pain of his withdrawal. He waved the white flag, in a matter of speaking.

I had seen a number of people, mostly patients with terminal diseases, surrender to their illnesses, so it's easy for me to tell when the end is approaching.

I rose slowly from my seat and exited the motel room. I wanted some time outside.

I wanted to listen to the cars produce speed on the nearby highway. I wanted to feel the soft breeze flirt with my face. A face that was unshaven for quite some time. I wanted to experience my atmosphere without hearing the agony in the bathroom.

It felt wonderful.

I went back to the room and returned to my monitor. The Subject had crawled to the bathroom door while I was outside. He was almost entirely without energy. Despite all logic, it seemed that he had made one last attempt to escape. The only thing he accomplished was exhausting himself.

There was only one thing left for him to do.

The Subject utilized the last drop of energy left in his purple body by grabbing a piece of broken mirror from the floor. Doing his best to combat his tremors, The Subject brought the shard of glass to his right wrist and sliced vertically, just how a suicide is supposed to go. Perfect technique.

He learned this method from the violent videos he obsessively showed The Bully. Back when The Subject and I were seeing the world through similar eyes. Now he was using those teachings to bring an end to his own torture.

It wasn't long before The Subject slipped into a permanent state of unconsciousness.

It happened like a downward flip of a light switch.

The Subject was dead.

The final word he mumbled was, "Again."

Uttering the word sounded like an unbearable process for The Subject. It literally hurt him to do anything. He sounded as if he had been stabbed with two knives. One in his heart. The other in his throat.

He then became nothing more than another corpse.

I tossed the furniture out of the way and moved into the bathroom. Upon entering, the stench hit me like a sledgehammer to the face. A sledgehammer dipped in piss, shit, blood and puke.

I have sniffed some unspeakable odors in my time, but my lord, when entering that bathroom I nearly contributed my own vomit. It was as if someone had shat out damnation.

I wanted to retreat.

I wanted out.

But I figured the longer I delayed the worse the situation would become.

I needed to quickly adjust to the scent and come up with a plan. I had no idea of what to do with The Subject's body. It was perhaps the first time in my experiment that I felt out of my element. I was highly indecisive.

I didn't know if I should run out to get cleaning supplies. Or get a saw and hack up The Subject. Or bag and drag the body to the car and bury it somewhere distant. I did not know where to begin.

I never had a chance to initiate any of those plans.

While I stood over the body, looking into The Subject's open yet lifeless eyes, a big bang sounded off, yanking me away from my focus.

I tried to argue in court that there was no knock on the door and, seeing as I was paying for the room, I figured the forcible entry was illegal. The judge did not accept that argument. He called it "nonsense" and "irrelevant."

The Judge said this as if he had just mounted an extremely high horse named Superior. Bollocks. Like his erroneous judgment could ever mean anything! Like his inability to see the truth actually mattered!

He was completely wide of the point.

The Judge saw me as a threat against humanity. He considered the police force kicking down my motel door justifiable.

Whether or not it was right (it was not!) it doesn't make a difference now. There's no changing anything.

The police force did what they did and came storming inside my room like I wasn't an esteemed Doctor.

It happened very fast. Once the door was kicked down, I heard an abundance of shouting. Then I was suddenly down on the bathroom floor, lying face to face with The Subject.

I began laughing when I looked at him from that angle. It was a good hearty laugh too. The type of laugh I hadn't enjoyed in many years prior to that moment. One that I haven't I enjoyed since.

The hilarity was interrupted when a great pressure formed on the back of my neck. This occurred due to one of the officers using his knee to hold me down. The pain was massive. I saw flashes of white and felt that I might pass out.

I'm very glad I didn't. Not because I'm concerned about fainting, but because I wouldn't have heard another officer mutter the words, "Jesus Christ."

He said it as if he was offended by what he saw in that bathroom. This made me ecstatic. I was happy to provide discomfort since him and his team should have never kicked down my door in the first place.

From his reaction I was also able to see that my experiment was truly special.

Innovation frightens people.

Next thing I knew my hands were cuffed and I was put in the back of a squad car. Like some wild animal.

The car sped to the precinct.

Upon arrival, the officers not only kept my hands shackled, they also chained my ankles to a chair. A chair cemented into the floor of an interrogation room.

The room was cold and bright.

I was very uncomfortable.

Two interrogating officers entered the room, but only after I was left alone for what must've been twenty minutes. The first thing they did was show me my old tracking device. The tracker I once used to keep tabs on The Subject. The goddamn tracker!

One of the officers explained that my former colleague had stuck it on the bumper of my rental car. This was obviously how the police were able to find me.

The officers said their only regret was that #1 got to them too late. According to the police, if #1 showed up sooner they would've, "saved that poor boy." The one I, "tortured".

I scoffed at the word torture.

As if they knew what really took place.

I would have explained that I was actually collecting cutting-edge medical information, but I knew the simpletons would not have understood. They didn't want to hear the truth. They just wanted to push their assumptions down my throat and try to alarm me.

In fact, when I scoffed at the mention of torture, one of the officers slammed his fists on the metal table between us and said, "You won't be laughing when you're rotting away in a cell."

I thought he was being overly dramatic.

I never figured he'd be correct about the cell.

I figured the moment I was in the courtroom I'd be able to properly explain my side of the story. I figured I'd be able to exhibit that I was only guilty of elevating the human psyche.

I figured it would be in that courtroom where I'd finally be applauded as a modern day Einstein or the second coming of the great Robert Gardiner Hill. But that didn't happen.

I never had a chance.

So much for the American Judicial System.

***

I defended myself in court. For a little while.

This was initially met with resistance since the magistrate thought I might be mentally deranged. But I was able to temporarily act as my own attorney once I proved my soundness.

I defended myself as well as I could. Quite cleverly, if I do say so myself. Not that it mattered. The prosecutors exaggerated "the evidence" in relentless fashion. They made me look so bad that, less than midway through the trial, the judge forced me to step down as my own attorney. The prosecutor's' lies convinced him that I was no longer capable.

They twisted and misrepresented all of my marvelous research. They made the jurors unanimously believe that I was a murderer, an accessory to murder, and an accessory to sexual assault, to name a few.

I was even hit with a kidnapping charge since the prosecutors said I deceptively adopted The Subject.

It was all bollocks.

But I'm smart enough to know what happened.

Every now and then, society feels the need to put a "monster" on display. They do this so they can publicly attack this person.

And why does society want to publicly attack?

Because it creates a feeling of unity (albeit a false one) and makes society feel warm and cuddly that the "monster" is locked behind bars.

Or, in my case, with padded walls and a straightjacket.

NOTE #15

KAREN: *Don't you think that society is...*

DR. RAVENSDALE: *It's time for you to leave. I'm done with your questions.*

In the Course of Time

Part of me doesn't want to write this section. I don't want people thinking that I'm trying to justify myself, or that I'm searching for redemption.

Absolutely not.

My actions are correct.

This section is nothing more than a simple reiteration.

I have no doubt that my work will be a major portion in the history books. I am positive that I will be remembered for a very long time. Da Vinci. Newton. Darwin. Ravensdale.

This is a foregone conclusion.

In due time, I will not be the man my contemporaries made me out to be. I am not a psychopathic demon. Everything I have done was for the greater good of humanity.

People will someday see this.

They will see the greatness I've achieved.

The biggest victory will come when the people of the future stand up to voice their disgust over my incarceration. Every wrong will be remedied. Those who have died for my experiment will eventually be seen for what they truly were: tools and devices. Not victims.

Yes! I will be seen as the genius who risked everything in the name of discovery.

This will happen!

I am not crazy.

I am the sanest man I have ever met.

I am not weak.

It doesn't matter that my mother was a prostitute.

It doesn't matter that I was bullied in school.

It doesn't matter that no woman ever loved me.

I put an end to that wretchedness.

Why?

Because I am strong!

I am Dr. David Ravensdale.

I am resilient!

I will never be broken.

Not even by the guard who entered my cell earlier today to tell me the "big news."

Yes, the big news.

I initially didn't want to write about this because I didn't want to seem affected.

But you know what; I am affected by it. In a good way.

The guard entered with a smirk on his face, feeling that he'd be able to dismantle my world. He leaned in and spoke loudly. His booming voice bouncing off the walls of my cell.

He told me that the results of The Subject's DNA examination came in and, after many additional tests to verify the outcome, The Subject turned out to be my son. My own flesh and blood.

What are the odds?

It's honestly magical.

The fact that I had a son isn't preposterous, given all the sperm I've donated in my life. But it's almost supernatural that my former colleagues found him as an infant. Particularly since he was discovered at an adoption center.

It turned out that after The Subject's mother became pregnant with my sperm she died due to complications with the childbirth.

It was destiny.

The guard thought I would be devastated by this news. Quite the opposite.

I initially didn't know what to feel. But as I was left alone, and time went on, I became thrilled.

Yes, I let my son die. There was no way around that. But his death didn't stop me from viewing the bigger picture.

The fact that I had one child means that I might have more. And this means they all have my blood. They have my viewpoints and ambitions and abilities.

They could be out there right now, feeling exactly how I feel. Being influenced by their heritage. Preparing themselves to continue what I started.

About the Author

Jeff Musillo is a writer, visual artist, actor, and director. He is the author of *The Ease of Access, Can You See That Sound, Snapshot Americana,* and *The Eternal Echo*. His paintings have been exhibited in galleries throughout New York, have been showcased in magazines in both the U.S. and Europe, and will soon be seen in the upcoming film, *In Case of Emergency*.

His work in film, as a screenwriter, director, and actor, has premiered at The Hoboken International Film Festival, The Jersey Shore Film Festival, and The Katra Film Series. His new screenplay, *In The Ring*, is currently in pre-production and set to shoot in 2016.

He lives in Brooklyn.

SB

A Strawberry Book
www.strawberrybooks.com